The Lesson—According to Kicks

Heine pointed the knife at her. "O.K., Lady Godiva, take off the blouse."

She stood motionless, unable to answer or move.

"Go ahead," Heine said. "Take that piece of nothing off."

The boy's shoulders slumped and he began to groan. "Brace, mister!" Bar shouted. He put a fist in the boy's gut, and the boy sank to his knees in the dirt, weeping helplessly. "O.K., green-belly," Bar said. "Stay there. Your turn comes next."

Dazedly the girl undid her blouse. Heine reached and yanked it off her shoulders. She stood there quivering, her pink slip plain and worn. Behind them, Manny began to cough. Johnny stood rooted to the place from where he watched.

"Let the straps down," Heine said to the girl.

"Please. Please . . ."

"Do what I tell you." Heine held the knife menacingly. The boy began to pray softly in Spanish.

She raised trembling fingers to her bare shoulders and slipped the straps over them. The top of her slip and her bra fell to her waist.

"Let her go," Manny whispered. "You ought to let her go now. Huh?"

"Let her go!" Bar shouted. "What are you so worried about, mister? We're just teaching these two juvenile delinquents a lesson. Don't you understand that, mister? We're going to teach these two juvenile delinquents a lesson they're never, never going to forget." He drew his foot back violently and kicked the boy in the groin. "Isn't that right, green-belly?"

The boy's scream of pain rent the air of the summer night.

The Thrill Kids

Vin Packer

PROLOGUE BOOKS

F+W Media, Inc.

Published in electronic format by
PROLOGUE BOOKS
an imprint of F+W Media, Inc.
10151 Carver Road
Blue Ash, Ohio 45242
www.prologuebooks.com

eISBN 10: 1-4405-3697-X
eISBN 13: 978-1-4405-3697-7

POD ISBN 10: 1-4405-5612-1
POD ISBN 13: 978-1-4405-5612-8

This is a work of fiction. Names, characters, corporations, institutions,
organizations, events, or locales in this novel are either the product of the author's
imagination or, if real, used fictitiously. The resemblance of any character to actual
persons (living or dead) is entirely coincidental.

This work has been previously published in print format by:
Gold Medal Books / Fawcett Publications, Inc., Greenwich, CT.

THE THRILL KIDS

1

When kids who are still wet behind their ears begin to worship
a new god named Violence, then
a city must sit up and take notice!
—*From "Delinquency Means Failure,"*
New York Daily Record editorial

WHEN THE BIG BLOND BOY stepped out of the shower
in the locker room of the City Boys' Club, a voice yelled,
"Hey, Kraut! Leave it on, will you?"

Naked and dripping wet, he walked through clouds
of steam to the benches where the voice came from, and
he looked down at a boy bigger than he was, who was
sitting there pulling off his socks. Both boys were sixteen;
both were tall for their age. Emanuel Pollack, the larger
of the two, looked at least seventeen, and his body was
more muscular, his voice remarkably deep.

"What'd you say?" the naked one asked.

"I said leave it on. I want to duck under for a quick
one."

"No. I mean, like, what'd you say before that?"

"I don't know," Manny Pollack said uncertainly.

"You want me to tell you what you said before that?"

"What's eating you? All I want is a shower."

"You said Kraut, Manny. You know? Kraut!"

"I'm sorry, Flip. I forgot."

5

"Yeah, like—you *did* forget. Like you didn't remember at all."

Manny Pollack stood up and unbuttoned his undershorts, letting them drop to the locker-room floor. He turned his back on Flip Heine and reached down for a towel. "I said I'm sorry."

Heine took him by the shoulder and turned him around. He had to reach up to do it, because Pollack towered over him. He said, "How long you and me known each other, Manny?"

"Years, I guess. Years. But for the love of Pete, Flip—"

"And all them years I been telling you I don't dig the moniker. Right?

Pollack gave an exasperated sigh, but he did not walk away from Heine. He stood there nervously, waiting. He tried to prevent the inevitable, whatever it would be (it was always different; Flip had a great imagination), by saying, "Look, the kids at school call you that and it's sort of catching, Flip. I can't help it if I slip now and then."

"School's out, man," Heine snapped. "School's been out a month."

A door slammed behind them, and another boy came into the locker room. Through the steam his form could be seen only hazily, as shadow-like he moved past them and stopped a few feet away. Manny glanced at him briefly, but Flip did not flinch. His eyes were still fixed on Manny. They were dark and narrowed and intense.

"What're you going to do, Manny, to make me know you're not going to slip again? Like, don't you want to do something?"

"Flip, gee. It's been a good afternoon. Why spoil it?"

"You spoiled it, Manny. You hung me up."

Pollack looked down at Heine and shuffled his bare feet restlessly. He shook his head. "I don't want to fight, Flip."

" 'D I ever touch you, Manny?"

The newcomer was watching them now. Pollack felt embarrassed and uncomfortable, looking over his shoulder at him and then back at Flip. The steam made the room sweat with moisture.

Flip never took his eyes from Pollack's face. He said, "Emanuel Pollack?"

"W-what?"

"I'm talking to you. Like, don't you want to make me know that you're not going to have any more relapses of the old memory machine, eh?"

"All right," Pollack said resignedly.

"You want to do something, don't you?"

"Yes," Pollack whispered.

"Speak up, Manny, or I'll think you're insincere. You're not, are you?"

"No."

"Say it."

"I'm not insincere," Pollack said. There was a tense silence, and then he added, as he knew he was expected to, "I want to do something."

Heine smiled and nodded. "Course you do," he said. "But what could you do that would show me, Manny? I wonder . . ." He scratched his head in a burlesque gesture of puzzlement, and finally he told Pollack, "You know only a downright dog would call a good man Kraut. Hmm? Don't you think only a downright dog would? Like, dogs go crawling around and they don't know. Wherever dogs go, they don't know and they go on all fours. Even if they want to take a shower, Manny. Hmmm? Understand?"

"Yes," Pollack answered. He hesitated. Behind him and Heine the boy who was watching coughed. Coughed or laughed? Manny did not know. He could hardly breathe in the steamy air. He looked down at Flip and Flip's eyes were on him. Flip had a cockeyed smile tipping his lips and he raised an eyebrow as if to say, "Well?"

Quickly, so that the words were jumbled together, but still plain to everyone in the locker room, Manny said, "I want to go on all fours to the shower for you, Flip. May I?"

"You may, Manny," Heine answered. "Manny, you may if you really want to."

Then as he did it, Heine did not laugh at him, but there was laughter. Laughter, and sudden applause. Before Manny ducked under the water, he heard a strange voice call to Flip, "Infinitely well done, sir! Huzzah!"

Outside the C.B.C. a half hour later, the midafternoon July sun was still hot as Flip Heine stood on the stone steps with his new acquaintance. The traffic on upper Lexington Avenue was sparse. New Yorkers had

deserted the city for a week end in the mountains or
on the Island. Flip mopped his brow with a clean white
handkerchief and glanced at his watch. Although he was
thin, his square-cut face was full and ruddy, and his nose
was pudgy. Strands of his yellow hair, which he wore
in a duck-tail haircut, kept falling across his forehead.
He habitually pushed them back with hands that were
childlike in their smallness. His lightweight trousers were
pegged and pale blue, with high risers and a navy-blue
suede belt resting down on his hips. His shoes were suede
and navy blue, too, the same color as his silk shirt with
the red diamond design on the pocket. The collar of
the shirt was turned up slightly. His large brown eyes
seemed restless and anxious as he looked expectantly down
Lexington Avenue, and when he said anything, he turned
his eyes from the boy beside him and talked to the sidewalk or the street. He mumbled his words, and his sen-
tences were thick with the slang of jazz, which he had
acquired in the past year, and which he broke into with
desperate spontaneity on occasion. Already he respected Bardo Raleigh.

"You'll like Wylie real fine," he said to him. "Him
and me and Manny hung around a long time together
now. Been in the same classes in school and everything.
Wylie works Saturdays till four, for his old man. Ought
to be along in a minute now."

Bardo was a somewhat short, well-built seventeen-year-
old. He had a good stance, which he had proudly per-
fected in Sandside Military Academy, along with excel-
lent manners, a sullen sort of sophisticated poise, and an
unusual skill in the art of fencing. His hair was dark
brown and combed back in a neat wave. He was a
nice-looking boy, not too handsome, but attractive in a
clean-cut way, with regular features and fine light-blue
eyes. His smile was particularly winning, for he had
good white teeth, straightened to perfection by braces
when he was a child. But one seldom saw him smile.
Bardo Raleigh believed that "smiling all over the place"
was "vulgar."

"It somehow is not feasible," Bardo remarked in his
contemplative, detached manner, "that you and your colleague inside would still get along after a performance
such as the one I witnessed."

"Manny's O.K.," Flip answered. "He goofs sometimes."

"Pardon me?"

"You know, man. Like, he shoots his mouth off."

"Peculiar," Bardo mused, "that he's so susceptible to sadism."

Flip shrugged his shoulders. He did not know exactly what Raleigh meant. He said, "He likes snakes. He has one and everything. One of his own, you know? Keeps it in his room. Man, I mean, who *needs* it?"

"Obviously he does," Bardo commented. "He probably has a psychological complex."

"He'll be along in a minute now," Flip said, looking back toward the club door and whistling shrilly at it. "Takes him a crazy time to dress," he added. Again he checked his watch, searching the street afterward for any sign of John Wylie. Flip had suggested to Bardo that he come along with the three of them, and Bardo had said fine, he would, but where were they all bound?

"The store," Flip had told him. "Down the street on Ninety-first."

"What store?"

"Bernie's. Like, they sell magazines and Cokes and they got a juke and couple pinballs and things. You know?"

"What are you going there *for?*" Bardo had inquired.

"*For?* You have to go *for* something? We're just going there."

He glared at Bardo with resentment. It was the same resentment he frequently felt toward his family. They couldn't understand why he hung around Bernie's either.

"You got records home," his old father would argue with him in German, "and you got a phonograph. And you got all the soft drinks you need downstairs in the place. Bring your friends home, Hans, the way a good boy does."

"The place" was Die Lotosblume, the Heines' small restaurant on Eighty-sixth Street near Third Avenue. Flip's sister sang there, and his three older brothers helped run the business. Four evenings a week Flip waited tables reluctantly, hating the familiar smells of grilled *Bratwurst,* red cabbage, schnitzel, and dark draught beer. The melancholy choruses of *"Muss I' Denn," "Lili Marlene,"* and *"Nur Du,"* which filled the room as the night wore on, filled Flip with shame at being there among the white-haired old Germans whose tears rolled down to their handle-bar mustaches as they reminisced; whole families gathered around one table, their napkins tucked under their chins, their voices rising in thick, guttural accents; and the sight-seers, who asked Flip what *Bauernwurst* was, what kind of meal a *real* German would order, and if the "little *Fräulein*" would sing "Come, come, I love you only" in German for a dollar bill.

"Aren't we good enough for you, Hans?" his father would demand.

"I didn't say that," Flip would answer.

"You say it, Hans. You say it with your eyes."

"O.K.! O.K.! I don't dig Germany. Germans don't give me kick *one!*"

"You go to that store to learn that talk, is that it? To learn to talk smart-aleck to your old father?

"All the guys go there, Pa."

"All the wise guys."

Bardo looked questioningly at Heine now, and with nervous irritation coloring his voice Heine said, "Like, we go to Bernie's and put out for a Coke, and play the juke. Bull around."

"Well, don't apologize, my good man," Bardo responded.

Flip had never heard a crazier comment in his whole life. Who was apologizing?

Wylie was ten minutes late already, and Manny, as usual, was dawdling. Ordinarily Flip would not have been bothered by these things, but this afternoon he was. He wondered what to say to Raleigh, and he wondered what kept him from crossing him off as a creep and just ignoring him. All the while he wondered, he strained for another likely topic of conversation.

He said, "Wait till you meet Wylie, man. Man, girls eat their hearts for breakfast over old Wyle!"

Bardo shifted his rapier to the other arm, took a silver nail clipper and file from his pocket, and worked with it on his hands, which were already immaculately white, the nails meticulously groomed. He was wearing gray linen trousers, and a white shirt under his charcoal-colored linen jacket. His necktie was inch thin, and striped black and blue. His academy graduation ring, which he wore on the little finger of his left hand, had a ruby stone that flashed its reflection in the gold handle of the rapier, jutting out from the leather case. Heine and Pol-

lack had gone to the club for handball, but Bardo had
gone there for his fencing lesson. When it was over
he had planned to drop the sword with the doorman
at his apartment building and go to a double feature.
Then in the locker room, when he got into conversation
with Flip, after Manny had dog-walked it to the shower,
Bardo had changed his mind. He was immediately cap-
tivated by Heine's disciplinary measure, and by the amusing, almost absent way he instigated it, and afterward appeared to slough off his triumph over Pollack. Such an
impassive personality intrigued Bardo, to say nothing of
the whole subject of discipline.

Raleigh had been an exemplary cadet during his four
years at Sandside. In that strange world of little men
carrying big guns, parading close order in full dress, standing white-glove inspection, and "popping to" like au-
tomatons at a senior officer's sharp bark, Bardo excelled.
During his four years at the academy he had been "pulled"
only once, in his freshman year, for failing to shine his
brass, and his last year he had served as Colonel of Cadets.
Discipline was his obsession. When he read in a modern history book one of De Gaulle's statements made
during World War II, he saw to it that every cadet mem-
orized it and could repeat it word for word. It was a
sentence that somehow inspired him:

"France will fight this battle with passion, but she will
fight it with discipline!"

"Thank God," Bardo had concluded his commence-
ment address on his final day at the academy, "that I
have learned the value of discipline, for it is the difference between leading and following in this world. The
followers will never appreciate its value; the leaders, who
do, are obliged to be their shepherds."

There was a polite sprinkle of applause from the stu-
dent-parent section, and a rousing ovation from General
Baird's box. The military band broke into the "March
of the Men of Harlech," and Bardo Raleigh did not touch
his glove to his cheek to stop the tear that had rolled
there from his brimming eyes.

"'How is it?" Bardo said to Flip, "that you have so
much power over your friend Manny?"

"I just put Manny down," Flip retorted. He disliked
analyzing situations. Flip just said things and people said

things back, and if it did not make intellectual history, it did not confuse him either. Bardo spoke unlike any-one Flip had ever encountered before. He seemed to probe for answers Flip did not know how to give him. It made Heine feel curiously and newly inadequate, and vaguely uncomfortable in Raleigh's presence. At the same time he was aware that he somehow admired him for this very fact. He was oddly pleased, even flattered, that Bardo was joining them.

"What do you mean, you put him down?"

"I don't like anyone calling me Kraut," Flip elaborated.

"I'm talking about power, my good man. Your *pow-er* over him."

"Power?" Flip shrugged his shoulders, embarrassed. "Who says?"

"Why *are* you so evasive?"

Flip chuckled and cracked his knuckles in a frustrated, awkward gesture. "Man, oh, man," he said, for no reason.

Raleigh said, "Where did you pick up that jargon?"

"Heard it around."

"He doesn't like it," Bardo said.

"Who doesn't?"

"Bardo Raleigh doesn't," Bardo Raleigh answered. "He finds it infinitely tiresome."

Emanuel Pollack pulled his olive-colored tie to a neat knot and studied his face in the locker-room mirror. He wondered if his father had been right this morning when he had suggested that the reason Manny had flunked two of his subjects this term was that the curriculum was too difficult for a young boy.

"They drive you kids too hard," he had said in his soft, serious tone. "They expect too much of you. Why, I saw you studying every night with my own eyes, Emanuel. Latin and French and all those subjects are *hard!* And you with an I.Q. of a hundred and eighteen. Nobody can say you haven't got the brains, Emanuel."

Manny would have liked to accept his father's idea that the school was to blame, and not himself, but Flip and Wylie both had passed their subjects, and he remembered the principal's report. His mother had read it aloud.

" . . . *convinced that his inability to concentrate and his dreamy attitude during class sessions are rooted in a basic personality problem. The faculty recommends that Emanuel apply for consultation with a psychologist at the Jewish Children's Clinic . . ."*

"You don't have to go, son," his father had declared. "You just forget all about it."

But his mother had said he certainly *was* going to go.

"Not if he doesn't want to, Ruth!"

"Well, he *should* want to!" and then turning to Manny she had said, "Don't you *want* help? Do you want to be backward and stay behind another year? You want help, don't you, Emanuel?"

"What about it, Emanuel? Do you?"

Emanuel said, "I don't know. I—What do *you* think?"

"I think," his father said, "that you should do as you please. You should do whatever *you* think is best, Emanuel."

As he remembered these things, Manny's reflection frowned back at him. His face was gaunt and somewhat sullen; his gray eyes were always rather timid-looking. A teacher once described Manny by saying that he had the face of a melancholy seventeenth-century poet and the build of a professional football tackle. His hair was chestnut-colored and curly, and now still wet from the shower. As he took his comb from his trouser pocket, he heard Flip's familiar whistle outside. Without bothering to part his hair, he grabbed the coat of his tan summer suit from the wire hook on the wall and began to run up the basement steps. Midway, he suddenly remembered the humiliating episode of less than an hour ago. It was funny that he had forgotten all about it, and funny too that as he recalled it, he was unable to recall his anger at Flip. The incident, he realized, was a dead issue, buried now in a graveyard of past and similar incidents.

Coming up Lexington Avenue, approaching the club entrance, Johnny Wylie wondered who the third boy was with Heine and Pollack. He saw Manny shaking hands with him while Flip stood by, grinning inanely and pushing the yellow strings of hair back off his forehead.

Johnny was the baby of the crowd; he had five months to go before he would be sixteen. He was five feet seven and clearly handsome, with thick black hair he wore close-cropped to his head, sparkling dark eyes, and a smooth, creamy complexion. Above his full wide lips he was cultivating a thin line of mustache.

"Where'd you get the 'tash, Johnny, hmm?" Lynn Leonard, the girl across the hall, had said shyly to him that morning as they met at the mailboxes in the apartment-house entranceway. "It's nice."

He had tried to keep his eyes off the tight white halter she filled too well for a girl of fifteen.

He said, "That's a funny name for it—'tash." He stared down at his shoes, afraid to raise his head for fear his eyes would never reach her face, but stay fixed there below her neck. He could smell the faint lilac fragrance she wore, and he was keenly aware of bare flesh at her shoulders and back, though he had not seen her fully.

"It's nice," she repeated. "It's a nice 'tash."

" 'Tash!" He feigned a gruff tone. "I never heard one called *that* before. Never!"

She laughed, tossing her head back so that her long, soft dark hair fell to the small of her back, and Johnny stole a glance at the halter. He looked squarely at her there, and then away quickly, his face flaming. He turned so she could not see.

"See you around," he mumbled.

"So long, Johnny."

"Do you stay in bed very long in the morning after you have once awakened?" Father Farrell had questioned Johnny after he had blurted out his confession twenty minutes ago, when he had stopped off at church on his way uptown.

"I won't any more, Father."

Johnny felt better now, after having talked about it with someone.

As if to dismiss these scraps of thought from his mind, he squared his broad shoulders, drew a deep breath, and held his head up high. He wore a brown cord suit and a natty yellow bow tie, which was clipped to the collar of his white shirt. The taps on the heels of his heavy oxblood shoes clicked more insistently as he stepped up his pace, waving now at the boys who were waiting for him. Johnny took the club steps by twos. He slapped Flip across the back and gave Manny a mock punch in the stomach. Then he shook hands with Bardo Raleigh.

"Let's all cut out for the store," Heine said, and as the sun slipped back behind the skyscrapers to the west, casting their jagged shadows in the path, the quartet ambled lazily along Lexington Avenue.

2

Hello, young fellow—hi!
You've got somethin' in your eye.
It's a look I recognize.
I don't think you realize
What's on your mind. . . .
        —"Love-Bitten"

Bᴇʀɴɪᴇ'ꜱ ʜᴀᴅ ᴏɴᴇ ʙᴏᴏᴛʜ, behind the magazine racks
in the back, and the four boys sat in it. Flip sat beside
Bardo, and Johnny and Manny faced them. All but Bardo were sipping Cokes. Bardo had heard that Cokes rot
your teeth. He had a cup of coffee. The jukebox was
playing the same song over and over and over: "Love-
bitten, smitten, smitten—sittin' in a daze . . ." Up front,
at the fountain, a lanky fellow with hair the color of a
carrot was blowing the paper wrapping from his straw
at a dark-eyed blonde who was thumbing through the
new issue of "Motion Picture." When the wrapper
whisked by her face, she looked haughtily at him over
her shoulder. She told him he should drop dead twice.
"The dog's barkin'," he said. "Somebody let her out.'"
Two girls straddling stools at the end of the fountain
swayed back and forth to the rhythm of the music, singing along with it: . . . "smitten, smitten—sittin' in a
daze . . ." Behind them three boys were jamming in the
levers on the pinball machine, making the bells ring
on a strike, and the red and yellow lights go on.
" 'And if I ever see you kick a dog again, mister,' I
told him, 'you'll pop to with this sticking in your yellow
gut!' " Bardo patted his rapier emphatically and took
a swallow of his coffee. "If there is one thing Bardo
Raleigh loathes," he concluded, "it's a yellow-bellied
bully!"
Emanuel Pollack said, "Particularly with an animal.
Geez, they can't even call for help or anything."
"You musta been a big deal at that academy, man,"
Flip said.
"I was a good officer, and if I get my appointment
to the Point, I'll be even better."

16

Johnny Wylie said, "What's 'pop to'? Is that when you stand up straight?"

"So straight you suck your belly in until it meets your vertebrae!"

"When will you know if you're in at the Point?" Flip asked.

"Any day now."

"Old Wyle here's going to Yale when we all finish up, and make like a lawyer, aren't you, John boy?"

"Not if I can help it!" Johnny said disgustedly.

Flip laughed. "If your old man can, you are. Least mine isn't on my back about college. I need college like a second head."

Manny said to Bardo, "Whatever happened to the guy?"

"Who? Yellow-belly? He's still at the academy. He has another year to go. I don't think he'll ever kick another dog during his lifetime, though. He learned his lesson." Bardo leaned forward, resting his elbows on the table. "We had this other cadet who used to pick on this homesexual. Whenever he could he—"

"You mean a fairy?" Flip said.

"If you prefer that word."

"What was he doing at the academy?" Johnny asked.

Bardo shrugged. "There are always two or three homosexuals in any school."

"Like, with the lily voice and the chicken walk and all?"

"Clayton didn't walk *or* talk too peculiarly."

"Then how'd you know?" Johnny said.

"Oh, everyone knew. He used to write poetry to men. I remember one called 'Song to Sydney.' The first line went: '*Haunch to haunch in our nude nakedness, we seek eternity . . .*' He used to recite it into a tape recorder and play it back. Then he'd erase it, change a few words, and start all over again. He said—"

"Haunch to haunch in our nude nakedness!" Flip exclaimed. "Dig that!"

Johnny grinned. "I know a joke about a fairy. This fairy gets his car bumped by a big truck, see, and he's sore as hell. So he gets out and goes back and says to the big, burly truck driver, 'Thay, what do you think you're *do*-ing, anyway?'—see? And the big guy says back, 'Aw kiss my butt.' So the fairy says, 'This is no time for love.

I'm mad!' " Johnny and Flip and Manny all broke into raucous laughter. Bardo just sat there.

"Don't you get it?" Johnny said. "This truck driver—"

"I get it, mister," Bardo answered coolly.

"Well, what's the matter? Not funny enough?"

"It was vulgar, mister. Kid stuff."

Johnny's face got red, and Flip spun a nickel on the table. There was silence for several seconds. The juke-box whined on.

"What happened to that Clayton?" Manny broke the silence. "You were going to tell us about him."

Bardo said, "It was just that one of the cadets used to pick on him, *bully* him. Homosexuals can't help what they are. They're born that way. But a *bully* isn't.

"You got something there, man," Flip agreed.

Johnny was quiet. He ran his fingers along his thin mustache and sipped his Coke with his eyes lowered.

"So one afternoon when this certain party was riding Clayton particularly hard, I decided to discipline him. I made him pop to and I said, 'Mister, there must be something deranged about you, the way you bully Clayton all the time. Maybe the trouble with you, Mister, is that you want to be a girl.' I said, 'Mister, if that's what you want to be, you can be.' Then I ordered him to put a hair ribbon on and get himself out on the parade field with a pair of scissors and a ream of bond. 'When you've cut yourself out a nice row of dollies from every single sheet in that box, mister,' I told him, 'you can come back to barracks. Then, mister.' I said, 'you can color them.' "

"Man, oh, man!"

"Did he do it?" Manny asked.

"You can bet your life he did it, mister."

"You must have been a big deal, man!"

Johnny Wylie stood up abruptly. "I have to go," he said. "It's five-thirty."

"I don't want to be a *big deal*, as you so vulgarly put it," Bardo said. "I simply want to be a man of some integrity."

"Be seeing you, Wyle," Manny said, noticing Johnny standing.

"S'long, Wyle," Flip said. "I'm not working next Saturday night. Want to cruise?"

"Sure," Johnny said. "I'll call you." He was about

to turn and leave when Bardo Raleigh stood, his hand outstretched.

"I'm glad to have met you, Wylie."

"Sure thing." Wylie nodded, taking his hand. He said good-by to the three boys again and started toward the front of Bernie's. As he passed the fountain, one of the girls perched on a stool called his name. .

"Oh, hi," he mumbled.

"Do me a favor, Johnny?"

"I guess."

"Put a nickel in Number Nine for me? Here," she said, holding the money in her hand. She giggled. "Look how red your ears get when you talk to a girl, Johnny."

Johnny said, "Put your own nickel in. I don't like the song."

"It's Number Two this week, Johnny."

"You think I watch the 'Hit Parade'?"

"Your ears are just scarlet, Johnny Wylie!"

"Give me the goddamn nickel," he muttered, "if you want to hear the song." He pulled it from between her fingers without touching them and turned to the jukebox. He shoved in the nickel and pushed the button. "Oh, oh, oh, oh! La'ove bit-ten! SSS-mitten!" The lyrics followed him out of the store, and the girl called after him, "Thank you, Johnny Red-ears. Much obliged for your courtesy."

"Lookit that." Flip nudged Raleigh when he saw John Wylie talking to the girl. "Man, dames are crazy about that cat!"

Manny said, "In school they all chase him."

"Aggressive women bore me," Bardo stated flatly. "I like my women to be passive."

"You—ever—" Flip stopped when Bardo met his eyes directly. Flip said, "I s'pose you got plenty of women."

"Only one, as a matter of fact," Bardo answered, rubbing the case of his rapier. "She's older than I am. She's a mature lady. I can't stand these ninny bare-legged kids."

"Ditto, man!"

"What's she like?" Manny said.

Bardo looked indifferently at him. "What do you mean, what is she like?"

Unsurely, Manny said, "W-what's her name?"

"Her name," Bardo said, pausing, drawing a breath, "is Ina."

"Oh."

"I-na," Flip sang softly, "is there anyone fina, in the state of Carolina? If there is, will you—"

"Kindly shut up!" Bardo snapped. "You're disagreeable, Heine!"

Heine stopped in the middle of a word and looked dumb-struck at Bardo Raleigh. Emanuel Pollack poured some salt out of the salt shaker he had been fondling in his hands, licked his finger, touched it to the salt, and tasted it, idly, feigning unawareness of the suddenly tense atmosphere.

"What'd I do?" Flip wanted to know.

"You act like a kid! I tell you a lady's name and you act like a kid!"

"I'm sor-ree!" Flip exaggerated the word. But he *was* sorry. He smoothed his hair back with his hands and then folded them across his chest. He looked at Manny, who was still intent on licking the salt off his finger, and he said, "You hung up, Pollack, you gotta eat salt?"

Manny stopped what he was doing without answering.

"Maybe you want to eat the whole shaker?" Flip said menacingly.

"I don't."

Bardo Raleigh kept Flip from pursuing it. "Don't bully him just because I told you to shut up," he said.

Flip got angry. "What's with you, man? Back at the club you're coming on like crazy 'cause I tell Manny here to do something and he does it, and now you sound off and say I'm bullying! What kind of an *academy* you running *now?*"

Bardo explained quite solemnly that there was a distinct difference between disciplining a man and bullying a man. "If he's out of line, then, mister, you discipline him. But if he's in line, you don't meddle. If you *do,* you're a bully."

Flip thought that over while Manny blew off some salt that was still sticking to his finger. Finally Flip said, "O.K. O.K."

"You see what I mean, don't you, Heine?"

"I said O.K."

"You're all right, mister," Bardo announced, "but you could use a little discipline yourself."

Heine was pleased. He saw more praise in the remark than blame. Reaching across the booth, he tugged playfully at Manny's tie. "Manny's a good kid," he said. "Me and Manny and Johnny gone around together since the year one."

Manny grinned and straightened his tie.

"Some night," Bardo Raleigh said, "we all ought to get together. What are you all doing tonight?"

"I can't make it," Flip answered. "I'm tied up."

"You working tonight, Flip?" Manny asked.

"I'm tied up's all. You want a diagram?"

"I didn't mean *tonight*," Raleigh said quickly. "I have something on myself tonight. Something important, as a matter of fact."

"Ina?" Manny said.

"Pollack, let me ask you something? Do you think you know me well enough to question me about my personal life?"

"I don't know, Bardo." Manny looked hurt.

"I don't think you do, mister."

"That's right, man. You don't," Flip agreed. "Bardo here doesn't ask me what I'm doing," he said. Flip was glad he didn't. It was his week to work at the place.

"I didn't think I was asking anything wrong," Manny said.

"Not wrong, mister. Simply familiar."

"Yeah, like you was Bardo's guard or something, man."

"Familiarity breeds contempt, mister. Remember that."

"That's good," Flip said. "You read that someplace?"

Manny had a baffled expression on his somber face. He had the top off the salt shaker now, and was poking his finger down in it, watching Bardo. From his inside coat pocket Bardo took out a notebook with a gold pencil attached to its side.

"Write your addresses down," he said, shoving the notebook to the center of the table. "I can contact you one evening when I'm free."

Flip reached out and scribbled his name and phone number in it.

"Write mine, too, will you, Flip?" Manny said quietly. To Bardo he said, "I didn't mean anything by it, Bardo."

"It was just poor taste," Raleigh responded.

"I realize that now."

"Forget it, then, mister."

Heine pushed the cowhide notebook back to Raleigh. He said, "I got to check, man. 'S late," and he looked up at the wall clock and said, "Jesus Christ, it *is* not early at all!" Still he sat there. Bardo was reading Heine's entry.

"I got to cut out," Flip said.

"I'll walk along with you," Manny said.

"You just wrote down your telephone number, Heine," Bardo remarked. "No address."

"I didn't have time. Man, like, I've got to cut. I'm late." Heine got up.

"You wrote Pollack's down."

"I'm only a few blocks from where I live now," Manny said. He was sliding out of the booth to go with Heine. "Going our way, Bardo?"

"I have a phone call to make," Raleigh told him. He stood and held out his hand. He gripped Manny's limp palm unexpectedly. He said, "Pollack." Then he took Flip's more certain hand. "Heine. I'll be in touch with you."

"Crazy!" Flip approved enthusiastically.

Manny said, "If I'm not home when you call, you can leave a message with my folks, and then I can call you back. Only I'm usually around. I'll probably *be* home."

"Good afternoon, gentlemen." Raleigh saluted them smartly before they turned and went.

After they had gone, Bardo tucked his rapier under his arm and strolled up to the phone booth. Pausing outside momentarily, he fumbled for change, found a dime, and stepped into the box, pulling the door to after him. He dialed ME 7-1212. A recording of the time played over the wire, once, twice, a third time. Bardo watched through the glass at the two boys playing the pinballs across from the booth. They were concentrating on their game, paying no attention to the phone booth. Bardo took his pencil out, the neck of the phone cradled between his chin and his shoulder. Quickly, but with care, he printed a four-letter word: "D-I-R-T." That was all.

3

He looks like the kind of boy
any mother would be proud of. . . .
—*Syndicated columnist Sheila Gage,
describing Emanuel Pollack*

SINCERE WAS EATING. He was a snake—a king snake—
and he was devouring a rat Manny had got for him that
morning. He was swallowing it whole, his green-striped
ebony skin stretching like rubber to take it into the canyon
of his jaws. Manny was standing there in his bedroom
watching him.

"You like to watch him eat, don't you, Emanuel?" His
mother's rasping voice suddenly threatened the still apartment. "It gives you some sort of pleasure to see him gulp
that little animal down!"

The boy kept his back turned on his mother. He said,
"He has to eat too."

"But you watch him!" she said. "You feel the way he
does—the way he is—vicious! *Sincere!*" She gave a mock-
ing little snicker. "Vicious is more like it! Cruel!"

She was a skinny, tired-looking woman who had once
been willowy and vivacious. There was the smoking stub
of a lipstick-stained cigarette between the thin fingers of
her right hand, and her left hand pushed back wiry black
hair that seemed never to be in place. Her dark-brown
eyes appeared sunken, and their expression alternated, ac-
cording to her moods, from dull and lusterless to bright
and mean.

Manny dug his fists into the worn pockets of his old
trousers and turned away from the cage he had built for
Sincere out of wood and wire and a pipe for water. He
kept his cage beside his desk, upon which were placed the
jars containing the bugs and beetles that were the snake's
food. Over the desk there was a picture of a boa he had
cut from the *National Geographic Magazine* and framed
himself, and on the opposite wall hung his brother's war
citation, also framed, and a picture of his brother. Scribbled across it in green ink was the inscription "For the
kid, for luck, and with love, from Irv."

23

Manny said, "What time's my appointment with Dr. Mannerheim?"

"You're going to change your clothes," his mother said. "You're not going in those filthy rat-hunting pants."

"What time she want me at her place?" the boy asked again.

"Five o'clock sharp," his mother told him. "Are you going to the zoo first?"

"I'm taking Sincere up with me. Man there's going to tell me how to get bugs out of his skin."

"Oh, my God!" his mother moaned. "Bugs out of his skin!" She shuddered and started from the room. Then she turned. "What are you going to do with the thing while you're at the doctor's?"

"Be in a box," Manny said. "Won't harm."

"Won't harm!" Her eyes squinted at him. "Won't harm! You just don't drag vipers along with you when you go to see a doctor, young man. Your father will have something to say on this subject. You think you can get away with murder, don't you?"

Manny did not say anything. A phone rang and then stopped abruptly. The cigarette in his mother's fingers fascinated him. It was burning down closer and closer to the flesh. She was looking at him, but he would not let his eyes meet hers.

She said, *"Don't* you?"

"I don't want to fight," Manny answered.

His father's voice, calling out, "Phone, Manny!" made it possible for him not to.

The Pollocks lived in a five-room apartment facing Madison Avenue in the East Nineties. Often, late at night, Manny could hear the uniform, rhythmic thumping of horses' hoofs on asphalt as the policemen rode into the Armory. When he and Irv were kids, they both had ambitions of becoming mounted policemen. Manny used to picture the two of them riding down Fifth Avenue on parade days, making the crowds stay back. He would think of how he and Irv would exercise the horses, running them around the reservoir in the early morning. And he would think of how they would play polo on the police team. Manny never thought of doing it without Irv. When Irv grew into his teens and announced suddenly one day that he was going to be an engineer, Manny was jolted into accepting a fearfully simple and awful truth: Nothing about the future could be guaranteed. The future, in a way, was like his father's answer to virtually every question: "It all depends." Irv began playing with a slide rule shortly after his decision, and he told Manny policemen didn't earn much money at all. He said that Manny ought to figure out something else to be, and it hurt Manny that his brother did not invite him to be an engineer too.

Now, whenever Manny heard the horses' hoofs, he wondered what to be.

The telephone was in the foyer. On his way to it, Manny passed his father, who was slumped in a worn leather armchair in the living room, watching an old Charlie Chan movie over television.

"Thanks, Pa," Manny said as he went by him.

"You're very welcome, son."

On the phone stand in the foyer there was Manny's father's copy of *The Jeweler's Trade Journal*, a glass paperweight with a picture of Irv magnified inside, and a thirsty ivy plant in a china pot shaped like an elephant.

After Manny said hello, it took him several slow seconds to realize who his caller was.

The voice said swiftly and succinctly, "Bardo Robert Raleigh extends a cordial invitation to Emanuel Pollack to attend a get-together this evening at eight o'clock, in his lodgings at Ten-eleven Fifth Avenue. Dress optional."

Manny said, "Oh, hi, Bardo," and became immediately aware that in the living room his mother was complaining about him to his father.

"Can he count on you?" Bardo asked.

"A party?"

"A get-together."

"Who's coming?"

"Messieurs Heine and Wylie, I believe. Others, perhaps."

". . . all seems so unfair!" his mother's voice whined. "They're as different as day and night. God, remember how Irving used to fix things around the apartment? Whenever—"

Manny said, "Sure, I guess."

"Ten-eleven Fifth Avenue. Eight P.M."

There was a click, and the dial tone came before Manny was certain that his conversation with Bardo Raleigh was over.

Lingering by the phone stand, Manny heard his father

say, ". . . shouldn't expect him to be like Irv. That's what's wrong with the world today. People expect everyone to be like *they* are. There's no chance for the individual. My father thought *he* should run his sons' lives, and look at us. Abe a jeweler, and me a jeweler, same as he was. No, Ruth, Manny's going to live his own life. I'm not going to live it for him."

"You're not living his life if you merely explain right from wrong!"

"What does the boy do wrong?"

"Nat, he's not passing his subjects! He has to go to a psychologist! He worships that crawling vampire in his bedroom! What more do you want?"

"They're hard on a youngster these days in school. I saw Manny study with my own eyes. They oughtn't to give a boy so much work, drive him so hard. He's just a boy. I say leave him alone."

"Well, it isn't what his principal says, and it isn't what I say. He's going to Dr. Mannerheim, and he's going to-day! And he's not taking that thing with him!"

"I'm out of this, Ruth." His father sounded weary. "I've always promised myself that if I had sons they'd do what they wanted to do. I wouldn't tell them. They'd have their own lives."

Manny knew what was coming next without even hearing it.

His mother's voice broke as she said it. "The way Irving has his life, I suppose!"

There was a moment's pause. Nathan Pollack replied softly, "He wanted to enlist. You knew that. He would have had to go anyway, eventually. Still, you blame me. You try to blame me for my own son's death."

At the familiar sound of his mother's sudden weeping, Manny sat down on the green hassock. He waited there until he knew she was gone from the living room, down to the bathroom. The sobs sounded farther away, and muffled. A door slammed shut. Manny heard his father sigh and the leather creak as he sank back in it, and the sound of the television was louder now, and he heard gunfire and a voice saying, "Ah, once again we meet, you and I. But you are dead, old man, aren't you?"

"Manny?" his father said to him as he passed him again on his way to his room.

"Did you hear it all, Manny? I suppose you did."

"Doesn't matter," Manny said.

"Your mother just can't get over it. She just never can!"

"Yeah," Manny said.

"And she gets all these crazy notions about psychologists and all. Manny, I want you to know something. Will you listen to your father tell you one thing?"

"Sure, Pa," Manny said. "Sure."

"Whatever anyone tells you, Emanuel, you do what you think. Emanuel, psychologists are just human beings themselves. They live in the same rotten world we live in. Their sons get killed in wars too. They have no corner on wisdom in this life. No one has. A person can only do what he thinks he should."

"Yes, sir," Manny said.

His father was a little thin man who looked too tired and wizened for his forty-five years. He seemed always to dress in saggy-kneed trousers of no particular color, and the same unmatching worn tweed jacket, which was too small for him. Whenever Manny thought of his father, he saw him always the same way. He would be bent over the workbench down at the store, dipping a tiny spring in gasoline, or humming off tune and peering with his round jeweler's glass into a watch. He would be smoking, and the ash of his cigarette would be dangling precariously, ready to fall. His father's face was yellow in hue, like some kind of mild-flavored cheese, and he had gone bald as a young man. His small gray eyes looked as though they had seen everything, and were no longer watchful. At the same time, Nat Pollock's patient, weary face held the expression of a man who was waiting for still more to happen, as if there were no end to the burden of living. "Live your own life, Emanuel!"

"Yes, sir."

"When I was a boy I always thought I'd be a doctor. Not one of these head-shrinkers like this Dr. Mannerheim, but a *real* doctor. A surgeon!" He held his hands out, looked at them, turned them over and back again. Then he dropped them to his lap in a gesture of resignation "Your grandfather had other ideas for me. That's why I'm where I am today."

"You make a good salary, don't you, Pa?" Manny was not sure.

His father was noncommittal. "A boy should be allowed

to choose for himself," he said. "I'll never interfere with what you want to do. Remember that, Emanuel."

"Yes, sir."

On the television set a man was trying to sell reconditioned vacuum cleaners.

"Another thing, Emanuel," his father said. "I'm your father, Emanuel. You needn't 'sir' me. I'm just your poor old father trying to help you get along in this world."

"Sure, Pa."

"You're a good boy, Emanuel. There's nothing wrong with you."

Manny said, "Thanks, Pa. I guess I'd better be going if I want to get to the zoo." His father did not answer him. Manny said, "I guess I better come home before I go see the doctor. I mean, I suppose I should come home and drop off Sincere." He waited, as though he anticipated some confirmation of the soundness of his decision, but his father only said, "Have a good day, son. Youth is to enjoy."

Manny walked down the long hall toward the end, where his room was. When he passed the bathroom he heard water running, and he knew his mother was wetting a washcloth to hold to her eyes.

Inside his room, Manny went over to the cage and looked again at Sincere. The snake had finished eating, and was gliding back and forth across the cage in a sinewy, unsettled attitude. Manny grinned halfheartedly as he watched him, and he said softly to the snake, "What's the matter, Sinny? Hmmm? Don't you know what to do with yourself? Isn't there anyone to tell you what to do with yourself, fellow?"

4

Q. What do you mean, it was a funny summer?

A. The whole summer was. Not funny ha-ha, but different, strange. . . . Everything was mixed up.

—From a psychiatric interview with John Wylie

Jill Wylie had poured the coffee at precisely the right moment, as she always did, so that as Richard came into the dining room it had just begun to cool. After he had put in cream, the coffee would be exactly the temperature he liked. The soft rolls wrapped in a napkin in the silver service tray were, Richard knew, fresh from the oven, baked that evening by Jill, without the aid of ready mixes. Because it was Saturday, even though he had been late for dinner and somewhat unsure that he would be there at all, he knew that there would be Boston baked beans in the chafing dish, made after his mother's recipe. Jill was that kind of wife. She knew he was a man who wanted things done in a certain way, and that was the way she did them.

"Hi, darling," Richard said, standing for a moment in the open doorway.

The candlelight from the silver holders on the table was shining on her hair, and the jade color of her soft wool dress blended with the green of her eyes. As always, the lovely dignity of her startled and amazed and pleased Richard. He had felt it the first time he had ever seen her, taking dictation in the law firm of which he was now a partner, and he felt it still.

When she had first begun to gray, she had not waged war on the fact of her forties, with rinses, dyes, or treatments, as so many other women Richard knew had. She had accepted it graciously, until now she seemed even more stately and serenely beautiful than she had been when her hair was coal-colored and bound back tightly to her head,

29

showing a profile Madonna-like in its perfection. The gray hair was cut short and skillfully curled around her face, making a kind of monk's cap. Her skin was like burnished ivory. Her mouth, somewhat small, was always pleasant and agreeable. Jill Wylie had never been possessed of a young girl's figure; she was a trifle broad and large-busted. At forty-three she had a body that Richard thought of as being fully developed, good, and somehow respectable.

Sitting across from her now, Richard shook out his napkin and said, "Johnny eat already?"

"He's been invited to a party," she answered. Then she added, "You look tired, darling."

"I'm not really," Richard said. "There were a lot of speeches that dragged on into the afternoon. I wonder why lawyers always have to make speeches, even when they don't get paid for them. Who's giving the party Johnny's going to?"

Richard Wylie passed his plate to his wife, holding it in hands that were large and square-fingered and capable-looking. He was a very tall man with gangling arms and legs, thick black hair that had grayed only at the temples, and an angular face whose features seemed all to jut out suddenly, starkly. He was a serious, thoughtful man who, as a student at Princeton, had been well liked without being popular, respected rather than envied, Richard but not Dick. Both he and Jill were the sort of people who were more easily acclimated to their maturity than they had been to their youth.

"Someone named Raleigh. Someone he just met, I believe," she answered.

"Raleigh who?"

"No, darling, Raleigh's the last name. A Barton Raleigh, I believe."

"Did he look over those catalogues I left on his desk this morning?"

"I'm afraid without much enthusiasm. He claims it's too early to be worying about what college to attend. He just isn't interested."

Richard said, "Delicious dinner, darling. It isn't too early at all. Has he left yet?"

"He's in his room. I think he's peeved. I told him we wanted him in by midnight."

"Quite right," Richard agreed. "And I want to talk with him before he goes."

Johnny was not in his room. He had gone up to the roof of the apartment house; he wasn't sure why. Dusk was breaking and Johnny was watching it.

The apartment house was on Ninety-first between Madison Avenue and Park. From where he stood, Johnny could not see the East River, but he could smell the water and hear the barge whistles toot. He could see the television aerials, clotheslines, and the myriad lighted rooms of strangers. He could see a few trees, and terraces where bushes grew. Johnny watched without seeing anything closely; he seemed to be waiting for something else, yet he was unaware of what it was, even when the roof door slammed, and he knew she was standing there behind him.

He did not turn and look around until she said, "Hot! Huh, Johnny?"

All summer long she had been wearing halters. This one was red, backless, with a neckline that dipped down to the crease between her breasts. Her black hair shone in the twilight. She had a beautiful young face with round, dark eyes, and lips that were not painted, but were pink and wide and moist. Her smile was shy, almost apologetic. Standing there, she sank her hands into the large pockets of her full black cotton skirt and curled her toes in her open sandals, and she looked at Johnny with uncertain wonder.

He said, "Yeah. Scorcher today. Going to get even hotter, I bet."

"It couldn't get hotter!"

"Why couldn't it?"

"I don't know, Johnny." She laughed.

"No reason why it couldn't," he said.

She stood beside him then, leaning over the brick wall, her white arms resting on its top. Always she smelled like lilacs.

"What are you going to be, Johnny, when you grow up?"

Feigning an indifferent tone, he said, "I might be a disc jockey."

"Really?"

"Sure. I listen to them late at night when I'm in—my room."

"I don't have a radio in mine."

"I got a lot of records, too. Millions. All the old ones. They're the best."

She raised her arms high in the air and stretched. He

could see her breasts swell up, and through the V of her halter he could see the white oozing of flesh that was lighter than the skin that had been tanned by the summer sun.

He said, "You know something, Lynn? You and me aren't such kids any more."

"I know it. Remember when we were? You used to run away from me whenever I wanted to play." •

"I was always like that," he said.

She laughed, leaning back against the wall. "You were so scared of girls. It was funny."

"Maybe I still am." Johnny's face got hot.

"Not of *me*."

"Not of any girl, really. Cripes! What's there to be scared of?"

"Did you ever—kiss a girl, Johnny? To see what it's like?"

"That's a dumb question!" he said angrily. "That's a dumb thing to ask a guy!"

"I'm sorry."

She looked sad and hurt, and she pushed herself away from the wall and walked a step away. His face was sullen and petulant. Neither said anything. She stood with her back to him, her arms folded, her hands rubbing her arms. Johnny looked at her hair. It was so long and soft. It could cover his face.

He said finally, "You don't ask guys things like that."

"I'm sorry, Johnny."

He said, "Aren't you cold with your bare back hanging out like that?" He sounded disgusted.

"It's hot," she said. "I'm hot!"

"Lynn?"

"What?"

"You mad?"

"Uh-uh."

"You got your back to me and stuff."

She turned to face him. He looked at her eyes, at her halter, and at her eyes again. "Lynn?"

"W-what?"

"Can I kiss you?" His voice was husky, his words thick.

"I—don't know," she said. "I don't know what it's like."

He walked to her until he stood before her. She was not smiling, and neither was he. In the street a fire engine sounded, but they did not hear it. It had grown darker, but it was still light.

He said, "Please?"

"Johnny," she said. "Johnny, you're—*trembling.*"

His arms were full of her, and as he kissed her he was surprised, and afraid, and glad of how much there was to her. He had never held a girl in his arms before, so he held her too tightly, as though his strength were necessary to keep her from falling, and his mouth on hers pressed hard. He heard her breathing and his own with a certain awe, and he felt her hair tickle his cheek, and he smelled her with excitement that was growing in him in a way he did not want it to. Then his hand happened suddenly on her breast, before he knew he had touched her there, and when she gave a fast little cry, he withdrew his hand, the fingers still curved from the roundness. She pulled away from him, and they stood apart. Immediately he realized that he had to go. He could not stand there like that.

He started to say something, but he did not know what, so he simply left her there, unsure of the look on her face, because her head was bent. He walked to the roof door, opened it, and went down the stairs.

"Is that you, Johnny?" his father's voice called out when he entered the apartment.

" 'S me."

"Where've you been?"

"No place," he said.

"Come in here, John."

"In a minute!" Johnny snapped.

"You march yourself in here right now, young man!"

"Can't you wait a minute, for cripes sake? I got to go to the head."

There was no answer, and Johnny went down the hall and into the bathroom. When he finally emerged and entered the living room, Richard Wylie looked sternly at him. Jill Wylie was mending a pair of Johnny's khaki pants, sitting on the low-slung gray couch under the goose-necked lamp. The room was very modern, all the walls lined with bookcases. In the places where there were not books, there were small marble statues of headless goddesses or thin-necked ceramic vases.

Richard Wylie tamped the dottle out of his pipe and regarded his son thoughtfully.

"When you came in just now, Johnny, I asked you where you had been."

"I was up on the roof, Dad," Johnny said.

"It wasn't an unreasonable question, was it?"

"No."

"And unless my questions are unreasonable, I expect a civil answer."

Johnny said, "I'm sorry."

"Did you glance through those college catalogues today?"

"Some."

"You have absolutely no enthusiasm about college, have you, Johnny?"

"I just don't want to be a lawyer, Dad. I like music."

"Johnny, the interests you have now are going to change —the same way your friends will change as you grow older. Now, there's nothing *wrong* about having an interest in music. There's nothing *wrong* with wanting to be a disc jockey. But with a law degree you can do anything—even those things."

"You're always trying to change me—change my friends. What's wrong with my friends?"

Jill Wylie said, "By the way, Johnny, where did you meet this Raleigh boy who's giving the party tonight?"

"I suppose there's something wrong with him," Johnny said.

"Your mother simply asked where you met him."

"Flip and Manny met him at the Club," Johnny said tiredly. "He went to the store with us after."

"Is there something bothering you, John?" his father said. "You're crabby tonight."

"Everyone's nagging at me, for the love of Pete." He looked at his watch. "I'm late now. Party began at eight."

"Where is it?" Richard Wylie asked.

Johnny sighed. "On Fifth Avenue, in the Nineties."

"Will you sit down with me tomorrow and go over those catalogues, John?"

"All right, Dad. All right. But I don't want to be a lawyer!"

His mother said, "Your father wants to help you. Listen to him."

"I *listen!*"

"Then that's a promise about tomorrow?"

"If it's so important to you, Dad."

"It's important to *you*, young man," his father answered. "Very well, run off to your party."

Johnny walked with heavy steps across the thick gray carpet into the hall, where he took his jacket from a hanger in the closet. He had his hand on the door when his father said, "Johnny?"

"What now?"

"Midnight," his father said. "Do you hear?"

"Me and Cinderella," Johnny muttered.

"And Johnny?"

"*Yes,* Dad!"

"Before you go, you might put that package on the hall table in your room. I passed Doubleday's on my way to the bus this evening, and I picked up that new Brubeck album for you. That was the one you wanted, wasn't it?"

Johnny hesitated before he spoke. Then he said, "Now, why'd you go and do a thing like that, Dad?"

"It's strictly a bribe, young man. I want you to get busy with those catalogues."

"You've got yourself a deal!" Johnny answered. His face relaxed, and he grinned.

5

These newspaper guys make me
seem like some kind of thug.
"Thrill killing"! I didn't get any
kicks out of it. I just didn't want
to be square!
—From a psychiatric interview with
Hans Heine

FLIP HELD HIS JAW where the old man had hit him.
He stood by the kitchen table, shaking, his face colored
with rage and shame, his eyes tearful.

"Look at it!" his father commanded in German. "Turn
the pages and look!"

"Pa, God, lay off! I don't want to look."

"You look! Look and leave the Lord out of it!"

Slowly Hans Heine's hand touched the paper-covered
volume of Night of Horror. He turned a page. There was
a picture of a woman with her clothes half ripped off her
voluptuous body. Her bare back was striped with bloody
whip lashes. She lay on a floor with her arms wrapped
around a man's trousered leg, and he looked down at her,
grinning, whip in hand. She was kissing his feet passion-
ately. He was promising, "You'll get more, baby. I'm going
to give it to you until you can't move!"

"Keep on!" Flip's father barked angrily. "Turn the
page!"

As he did so, Flip looked through eyes that were brimming with tears at illustrations of scantily dressed, sensual
women being burned with cigarettes, strangled with wire,
kicked down long flights of stairs, tied to wheels, and
beaten with wet Turkish towels. His father watched him.
He was a large, fat man in his late sixties, with a bald
head that was red and shining, round dark eyes that
flashed his fury, and a small mouth, which was now tight
and tense. When Flip spoke to him, he spoke German. In
the Heine household English was seldom used, save when
visitors who knew no German were present.

Flip said, "What does this *prove*, Pa—making me do
this?"

"It proves you look at this trash. You spend good money
to look at this trash! Well, look! Look! Filth!" Again his
father struck him across the jaw. "Dirty son! Spend money
on filth!"

Flip reeled, regained his stance, and stood crying openly,
his shoulders heaving with his sobs. He could hear his
mother say, "No, Pete. No. Don't hit him more. It is
enough." She sat in the parlor beyond the kitchen, in a
straight-backed chair, her black shawl wrapped around
her even though the night was hot and muggy. She was
a little woman, plump and short. Her small face was dominated by bifocals, and her hands were perpetually knitting,
in an unceasing, automatic way. The apartment above *Die
Lotosblume* had five rooms that followed one after the
other, in a straight line. There were no doors to the rooms,
only curtains. Flip and his middle brother, Fritz, shared
a bedroom next to the one his older brother, Bob, and
his wife slept in. Beyond that one was his parents' bedroom. His sister and her husband lived a block away, on
Eighty-seventh Street, and his third brother lived with his
wife and kids in the apartment building next door to the
restaurant.

"You keep out of this!" Pete Heine warned his wife.
"You are too soft on this boy. He is a bad boy!"

Flip blew his nose and rubbed his handkerchief over his
wet face.

"Where did you get this?" his father demanded, pointing to the book.

"Some guys," Flip said. "I don't know."

"At the store? The store you love so?"

"No, pa. No!"

"You go there no more! You stay home. Work more at
the place. The devil has your idle hands!"

"I didn't get it at the store! Blame the store for everything!"

"You get a haircut! You don't look respectable!"

"All the guys—"

His father struck him a third time. "I say you get a
haircut, you get a haircut, Hans!"

"Yes, sir."

Flip's nose began to bleed. He held his handkerchief to
it to catch the blood.

"Blood," his mother muttered from the other room.
"Blood, Pete. Please—no more." She sat knitting, her

hands nervous, her own eyes filling. She said, "Hans, Hans, what can become of you?"

"Now!" his father said. "Go now to the barber!"

"Yes, sir," Flip said. "I got to stop the bleeding."

"You go now!"

"I want to wash my face, Pa. Please, I——"

"*Now!*"

"Yes," Flip said, hurrying, holding the handkerchief still to his nose. "Yes." He went past his mother in the parlor. She reached a hand out and touched his trousers and said his name in a tired, sad way. His father stood, arms akimbo, watching him. Flip opened the apartment door.

"Hans?"

"Pa?"

"When you come back you work tonight! You don't go anyplace tonight!"

"Pa, I was invited to——"

"I invite you to work! You come back here and you work in the place!" He slapped the paper-bound book to the floor. "Filth! You dirty son!"

Flip shut the door behind him and started down four flights of rickety wooden stairs. At the landing he reached into his pocket for his comb and ran it through his hair. He stood with his head back, swallowing the blood that came down his throat. When at last he put the handkerchief back in his pocket, he spat on his fingers and touched them to his eyes.

It was still light in the streets and he looked in the window of a florist shop to see the time. Seven. The barbershop was on the corner, and he went on past it.

For a long time Flip walked without knowing where he was going. He had an hour to kill before he would go to Bardo's, and the only thing he was certain of was that he *would* go there. All week he had thought about it, planned it, even saved out a shirt he wanted to wear. Now he was wearing one with blood on it. He hated his father. Every time he got a chance to climb another rung up the ladder leading out of Yorkville, his father held him back. Their differences always circled around picayune issues that developed with the suddenness of a thunderstorm in August, and lasted far, far longer. It made Flip burn to have the old man raise such a furor over a book like that. Flip had seen plenty worse up at Leemie's, where he'd got that one; the one he got was *nothing*.

When he cut across Ninety-eighth Street going toward Park Avenue, Flip knew he was heading for Leemie's store. He could get a fresh shirt from Leemie, maybe. Leemie was a creep *one*, but he had a way of getting things. Some of the things he could get were fantastic— all the dirty books and pictures, and bull whips, and things Flip sometimes didn't even know what a person did with. He pushed a little, too, Flip thought; not just "pot," but the real stuff. Leemie had his own monkey on his back. Flip smirked when he remembered the way Leemie sang: "I get my kicks from cocaine. Mere alcohol doesn't thrill me at all . . ."

The store was on the bad end of Park Avenue, up in the Hundreds under the New York Central tracks. Flip used to go up to the fruit and vegetable market nearby to buy for the place sometimes, and he got into the habit of stopping off at Leemie's to listen to records. Leemie sold sheet music and songbooks too, but he never sold very much of anything on display. It was his "front." Leemie knew all the latest jazz lingo, with some jargon peculiar to dopeys thrown in, and Flip liked to listen to it and memorize it. Even though Leemie was a little squirrily, no one could say he was square.

When Flip got there, the store was empty except for Leemie. It would be hard to guess Leemie's age. He was probably over thirty-five, but how many years over was not plain. Medium-sized, with a thin, sallow face, horn-rimmed glasses, and a hook nose, Leemie looked good only when he smiled, and then he looked a little silly too, a little "high."

"How come?" he said to Flip, who never came around in the evening to see Leemie.

"You mean me being here? Or this?" Flip pointed to his shirt.

Leemie shrugged.

"Well," Flip said, "I'm here to get another shirt, if you got one. My old man decided to play house tonight."

"Nice," Leemie said. He tossed a key ring at Flip. "Up one on the left. Two-B. You'll see the dresser."

"When'd these come in, Leem?" Flip's eyes ran along the counter. There was a cigar box filled with knives, all switchblades.

"They were never out."

"What do you soak?"

"For you? Two and a quarter."

"Can I charge?"

"Somehow that doesn't move me."

"Until Monday. I come up on Monday. Pay you then."
Leemie thought about it.

Flip said, "I'll bring the shirt back then too, and pick up
this rag. I'll pay you, Leem. I got to get a haircut with
what I got on me."

Leemie said he didn't mind.

Flip pulled a few of the knives out of the box and
looked them over, then tossed them all back but a black
one. He pressed a button on the side of the knife and the
blade shot out, sharp and gleaming.

"Don't goof with it," Leemie told him. "They aren't in
favor with the Fridays."

"It could kill a person," Flip said. "Like, lookit how
long that blade is. Man!"

"Got some new literature, too. Illustrated from real life."
Leemie laughed. He socked his fist up at his wrist in an
obscene gesture. Flip laughed too.

Leemie said, "In this one they're giving this girl this
enema, see, and at the same time—"

Leemie told Flip all about it. When he was finished,
neither one could stop laughing for a long time.

"You got time?" Leemie finally asked. "I'll let you look
at some of it."

Flip looked up at the clock on the wall of the small
store. It was twenty minutes to eight. He was going to be
late getting to Bardo's. He still had to get his hair cut. It
was going to be bad enough not to show up for work, but
to show up later without his hair cut—murder!

"I can't," Flip said. "I'll see them Monday. Where'll I
leave my shirt?"

"Bed. Bring mine back. *And* the money."

"It's a swell knife, all right." Flip had been holding it
the whole time, pressing the button and watching the blade
spring, pushing it in and pressing the button again. He
folded it now and put it into his pocket.

Leemie said, "You didn't get it from me if you goof."

"You kidding?" Flip said indignantly. "Think I'm
square?"

The shirt Flip found in Leemie's drawer was like no
shirt Flip had ever seen before. It was neat; crazy. It was
some kind of shiny material; not silk, but soft like silk, and

bright yellow, sun-colored. It had a wing collar, buttons covered with the same material as the shirt was made of, and five buttons on the sleeves. The best thing about it was the breast pocket. It had a heart on it, a big black one.

Flip studied his reflection in Leemie's mirror. He knew he looked sharp. He winked at his reflection and as he did so his eye caught one of Leemie's photographs of naked women. It was a glossy five-by-seven, stuck there in the corner of the glass. Flip went closer and stared at it with a dull, expressionless face. His hand went to his pocket where the knife was, and he drew the knife out fast, the blade bare and pointing. He swung his arm in a half circle until the knife just met the woman in the picture. He waited with it poised there, the tip of it nicking the surface of the photograph. Then he plunged it in. "You move me not at all, baby," he said, "but I sure kill you!"

6

Q. Who is Ina, Bardo?
A. Ina who?
Q. You mentioned her to the others at one time. Do you remember? You said she was your girl.
A. Lady! She is a lady! Do you think a gentleman would divulge a lady's name?
—*From a psychiatric interview with Bardo Raleigh*

THE RING was always kept on the right-hand side of the top drawer of the bureau in his mother's room. Bardo considered it ironic that such a cheap piece of ten-carat gold should be encased in a fine velvet box. Often, while his mother was sitting at the dressing table putting on the finishing touches of her make-up, Bardo would play with the ring. He could remember very little about the man who had given it to her. Bardo's father had died when he was not quite three. What he could recall about Thornton Raleigh was mostly inventions of his imagination, inspired by things his mother said about him from time to time. Things like:

"He was brilliant, Bar, but he was a little lost boy. He'd lose a button on his shirt and never notice it. . . .

"Some people can take liquor, others can't. Thorn couldn't. It was stronger than he was. It finally killed him. . . .

"Aw, Bar, there was a lot wrong with him, but he was a lovable bum."

That Saturday evening, before Flip and Manny and Johnny were to arrive, Bardo stood by the bureau where he could see the ring's case in the open drawer. His mother sat at the dressing table, brushing her hair. Her hair was light brown, feather-cut and softly curled. She had a wide mouth with lips that were soft and curving, and large eyes the same blue as her son's. They looked as if their owner possessed a delightful secret that could not, unfor-

tunately, be shared with anyone. There was not a single
feature of her face that was not exactly right, and com-
bined with her trim, well-molded body, with its slim, long
legs and full, ripe breasts, she made a wonderfully impres-
sive appearance. She had married too hastily, too young,
and she had never remarried after the sudden death of her
husband. She was thirty-five. Men who saw her on the
street turned and stared as she passed, and they said to
themselves and each other, "There goes a beautiful
woman."

Beauty, in a sense, was her business, and she aptly per-
sonified the title of the magazine on which she had worked
for thirteen years. She was now an associate editor at
Beautiful Lady. At work, she wore a hat; usually the kind
of hat other women would shy from buying, fearing themselves not quite dramatic enough for it. Her clothes were
always in good taste, but they were never ordinary either;
never the sort *anyone* would wear. Few would or could.

She was a woman who had worked hard for everything
she had, and "everything," to her mind, was Bar. Immensely proud of him, she was both amused and bemused
by him, and at times the only thing she seemed to understand about him was her love for him; yet nothing Bar
did or was met with her disapproval. She believed that
she would be quick to censure him, and equally quick to
forgive him, should the occasion arise, but it never had.
Aware that he was certainly different from most boys, she
accepted the difference without being able to define it.

"I just can't see Bardo at a baseball game, yelling his
lungs out for his favorite team," Claude McCoy, her most
enduring and persistent suitor, had once remarked.

"He'd think it was vulgar," she'd agreed, laughing.

She saw nothing remotely offensive in the statement.

Now as she saw Bardo behind her, through her mirror,
she smiled. Despite the sophistication he had cultivated in
his four years away from her, he still toyed with her jew-
elry as he had done when he was a little boy; and still he
stayed close to her, watching her prepare dinner in the
kitchen, following her from room to room.

He had begun calling her by her first name several years
ago. He did it in a kidding, affectionate way that she
thought of as cute. That, and his habit of referring to
himself as "he," were affectations that diverted and somehow pleased his mother. She was at first surprised and

then gratified to realize that Bar was interesting, quite apart from the fact that he was her son.

"Bar?"

He put down a box he was holding in his hands, and his eyes met hers in the mirror. "Hmm?"

"What are they like, the boys who are coming over this evening?"

"Oh, Ivy, I don't know. I guess you might say they're younger than I am. Not just in years, you understand." He crossed the bedroom and sat on the edge of her bed, opposite her.

Ivy Raleigh said, "Do you know them well?"

"No, I told you I just met them a week ago. One of them is something of a zoot-suiter. Most amusing."

"And the others?"

"Typical, I would say. Ingenuous."

"There. Do you like the way Leo cut my hair this time?"

"Very agreeable, yes."

"It's not too short?"

"Perfect!"

"Pearls or rhinestones?"

"Let me see. . . . Pearls."

"I think so, too. Pearls it is!"

He stood and walked over to the window, pushing the draperies aside so he could see down into Fifth Avenue. He looked across at the Park side, where there were benches spaced at intervals in front of the stone wall.

"Peculiar how they loiter," he said, nodding toward the people who sat idle on those benches. Then he said, "Do you think you'll ever *marry* Claude, Ivy?"

"Should I? I don't know. I'm fond of him. I always said I'd wait until you were graduated."

"He doesn't like me, does he?"

"Darling, don't be a silly goose. Of course he does!"

"Not very well, he doesn't," Bardo mused, watching one person in particular from the window. It was a man stretched out on one of the benches, apparently asleep. "Only because of you," he continued.

"That's not true, Bar."

Distracted momentarily, Bardo observed, "The police never patrol Fifth. Vagrants just lie around down there." He was frowning as he stared out.

"What makes you think he doesn't like you?"

"Intuition."

"Oh, *darling!*"

"He's jealous."

"Jealous!"

"It's infinitely feasible. We're so close."

"Claude isn't like that."

Bardo shrugged, still watching the man who slept on the bench. He said, "They're like cockroaches, these vagrants. In the dark they crawl out of the woodwork. Night comes and there they are. Eyesores!"

"It's this weather," Ivy said. "It's too hot for people who live in dilapidated buildings to stay indoors." She finished fastening the tiny pearl earrings to her lobes.

"Even in winter they find their way to those benches. And they're dirty. They're unbelievably dirty!"

Ivy stood up and turned before the long mirror on the back of the closet door. The deep olive-green dress she wore hugged her body tightly; the front and back of it dipped low to reveal a soft white back and bare chest to the gradual round rising of her bust, where a heart-shaped pearl pin was clipped to a side of the dress. Her hips curved out generously from her slim, pinched waist, and the straps of her open-toed slippers wound around thin ankles.

"You know, you really haven't any grounds for believing that, Bar, darling," she said as she looked at herself, turning to see her stocking seams. "I wish you didn't."

He whirled around, his eyes suddenly alive with intense concern. "Ivy, good Lord! A bum is a bum in any season, and he's filthy, and he reeks! I can smell a bum when I see him from the window! Foul-odored and unkempt! Clothes falling off him! What would you have me do? Sympathize with a filthy—"

His mother held her hand up, interrupting him. "No, no, no, no, honey! I don't mean about vagrants. I mean about *Claude!*"

Bardo looked vaguely disappointed.

"Oh," he said flatly. He walked away from the window. "Are you still on that?" Sinking his hands into the pockets of the gray cord trousers he wore, he regarded his mother. The frown on his face went, and his features softened.

"I just want it clear, honey. Claude *does* like you."

"All right," he said. "He does." He smiled. "Ivy, Bardo Robert Raleigh thinks you look utterly lovely."

"My darling," she said. "Thanks."

"Infinitely stunning." He stood there while she walked over to him, her hand touching his cheek. "Bar, you're very sweet," she said.

"And you're the only lady B. R. Raleigh knows."

"Thanks, darling. Hey, say—I'd better get those Cokes on ice. Do you know it's practically eight? Good heavens, your friends will be here."

She started from the room as Bardo said, "Not *friends*."

"What, darling?" She was already in the hall outside the bedroom.

"They aren't friends," Bardo called after her. "Merely acquaintances."

Ivy Raleigh went through the living room into the kitchen. The apartment looked deceptively spacious. Although it actually was a small flat, it was not an inexpensive or even a moderately expensive one. It was more than Ivy could afford, yet like so many things, she miraculously managed to afford it. Claude was right when he said, "You know it's ridiculous for us to live apart this way, Ivy. You killing yourself on that job to maintain this place, and me with a good-sized house in Clifton that I'm never in. Except of course *this* damnable summer. Why don't you marry me? Or at least let Bar face the facts of life?"

"Oh, he knows about us, darling," she'd answered.

"He knows we *go out* together."

"Do you think that's all?"

"I'd swear to it."

"It's funny. I really don't know. . . . But in either case, I dislike indiscretion of *any* kind."

"Then for Christ's sake, marry me."

"You know?" she had answered. "I might."

Before she had met Claude, three years ago, Ivy had shunned the idea of remarrying. At Thorn's death she had found a job that paid forty-two dollars a week. She moved back with her parents in Yonkers, taking little Bar with her. Thorn had left her with nothing but debts, and scarcely any good memories. The fact that she had loved him completely every day he was alive, and long after he was dead, did not alter the insurmountable fact of his failure as a husband and a father.

Marriage no longer seemed a profitable goal, and for it she substituted success in a career. But when she found Claude McCoy, she found also that her career was instantly and infinitely less important to her, and that

Claude was incredibly more a man she could love than Thornton Raleigh had ever been. When she became sure of this, Bar was in his junior year at Sandside. Out of fairness to him, she thought, she would wait until after his graduation and until his plans for the fall had solidified before making any decisions about her own future.

It was curious, she realized, as she set the Cokes in the refrigerator and covered the sandwiches she had made for Bar's friends, that he had mentioned marriage that evening. He had never done it before. Curious, and coincidental, for even that afternoon she had thought of gradually introducing the subject into their conversations this summer. Whatever it had been that had caused him to think of it, she decided, it was fortunate. Typical, too— for they *were* very close, and in the long run her son was not the enigma she sometimes imagined he was. In the long run, he was as transparent as any son is to his mother.

From the bedroom, where he was once more standing at the window, watching the bum on the bench, Bardo heard the doorbell. It was the downstairs bell, and he heard Ivy press the button that unlocked the entrance and call out, "Bar? Better come along. Your friends are here."

"Directly!" he answered. But he did not hurry.

For a moment he stayed peering down. His eyes were unblinking, their expression bland. Only an almost indiscernible vein pulsing near his neck belied his calm appearance. When he finally did turn away, he stood for another moment unmoving, looking now at the open bureau drawer. Then, going quickly to the bureau, he removed the box in which the ring was enclosed, and put it in the hip pocket of his trousers. Carefully closing the bureau drawer, he walked from the bedroom. There was a new spring to his step.

7

Hello, young fellow—hey!
Are you feeling strange today?
Do you wonder at the way
Everybody seems to say
What's on *your* mind?
—*"Love-Bitten"*

MANNY WAS THE FIRST to arrive, at three minutes after eight. He sat forward uncomfortably on the edge of the straight-backed chair in the Raleigh living room, rubbing his hands together. He wore his best suit, a thinly pin-striped cord, pressed and clean. Actually it had belonged to Irving, but Irv had worn it only once or twice before he enlisted, and after he was killed it had been cut down for Manny. Whenever he put it on, his mother invariably said the same thing: "I remember the day your brother and I went to buy that suit. Afterward we ate chow mien in Longchamps, and saw 'The Big Sleep.' Humphrey Bogart was in it."

Manny straightened his carrot-colored clip-on bow tie and cleared his throat. He sat dumbly while Bardo settled himself back on the couch opposite him.

"What's the matter?" Bardo asked him. "Are you nervous?"

"Uh-uh. I mean, no."

"Take it easy, then."

"I guess I'm early."

"No, you're not, mister. You're on time. You're on time. I like punctuality. It shows self-discipline."

"You said eight," Manny said.

Bardo took his silver nail clipper and file from his pocket and worked on his fingers as he talked. "I understand you like snakes, Pollack."

"I've got one."

"That's what I understand."

"I call him Sincere."

"May I ask why?"

Manny shrugged, grinning a little, blushing in a pleasant way. "I don't know. I guess because that's the way

48

he looked to me. He was in this box poking around in the grass, as though he had to hide himself or something, because people in the store there said, 'Oh, look—eeee!. A snake!' You know how people are."

"Infinitely immature," Bardo said. "The snake is one of God's most graceful creatures."

"People think they do harm," Manny said, "but they don't. Kinds like Sincere—the kings, and kinds like bulls and milks— they *help*. I mean, they eat rats and mice and things."

Bardo said emphatically, "Exactly! They rid the world of many filthy rodents. They move swiftly and surely upon their prey, and they kill with dignity."

Manny leaned back in the chair and crossed his legs. "You know," he said, "most snakes really walk on their ribs. They grip the ground with the sharp edges of the scales on the lower sides of their body. It's the muscles inside that pull them along the ground. Did you know that?" There was a short silence then; Bardo was paring his nails with the clipper, not looking at Manny.

Manny said, "I get too wound up, I guess, when it comes to snakes."

"Not at all! You ought to be a herpetologist, Pollack. You seem infinitely interested in herpetology."

"Thanks." Manny smiled. He paused before he spoke again. "That's someone who knows all about snakes, huh?"

"An *authority* on them."

"I wasn't sure. I thought that was probably it."

"You really ought to be a herpetologist, mister."

"I never thought of that. I mean, it just never occurred to me I could do something like that. Around snakes and all." Manny crossed his arms on his chest, his face alert with the expression of one who has made a significant discovery. "Gee, Bardo," he said. "Maybe I will!"

"Of course you will, mister!"

"I just—never—*thought* of it," Manny said, as though he were talking to himself now. "It never occurred to me."

Bardo continued to discuss the snake, dwelling again on its value as a killer of filthy rodents, but Manny sat only half listening, off on a flight of fantasy. He imagined himself telling his mother and father, Dr. Mannerheim too: "Well, I've made up my mind I'm going to be a herpetologist." He was still thinking of this when Ivy Raleigh came into the living room.

"Pop to, mister!" Bardo said.

Surprised by Raleigh's sudden terse tone, Manny looked across at him, and saw Bardo on his feet.

"Pop to!" Bardo barked again. "A lady is present!"

Manny stood up slowly, uncertainly. Ivy Raleigh was smiling, moving forward to take his hand. "Hello, there," she said. "You mustn't let Bar order you around. What's your name, dear?"

"I don't mind, ma'am," Manny answered. He took her hand and pumped it awkwardly. "I'm Emanuel Pollack." He wondered why he felt like adding, "I'm going to be a herpetologist."

"What would you like to drink, Emanuel. Coke? Ginger ale?"

"I don't know," Manny said. "Whatever's easiest."

"They're both easy. What'll it be, hmmm?"

Manny said, "Gee, I don't care. I—"

"Coke rots your teeth, mister," Bardo announced. "Have ginger ale."

Ivy chuckled, winking at Manny. "That's just *his* theory, Emanuel. You have what you feel like having."

Pollack hesitated. Then he said, "I guess I *will* have ginger ale, if you have plenty."

Claude McCoy was eager to begin this evening with Ivy, but he knew he would have to wait in the elevator of 1011 Fifth until old Henry was good and ready to take him up. He did not really mind the wait. McCoy was not an impatient man. Other men hurried, and they often stumbled and fell and frequently were unable to right themselves. Other men's grasps exceeded their reach. McCoy's did not.

"Do it slow and do it sure" was his motto. The words were typewritten on a piece of release paper that hung above his desk in the U. P. offices of the News Building.

"Hell of a motto for a newspaperman!" a colleague had cracked once. "Speed! That's the motto for a guy in this business."

"You're still green," McCoy had told him. "Someday you'll stop fighting the wire. Someday *you'll* be the wire's boss, and some skin'll get a chance to grow over those raw nerves."

McCoy did not believe in being neurotic. He believed a man ought to pull himself up by his own bootstraps when he was down, and he didn't believe there was any man who couldn't if he had the guts. Associates of his who paid half of their salary every week for visits to a psychiatrist did not command Claude McCoy's respect. He was unable to fathom why they were not able to help themselves. One of the reasons he was first attracted to Ivy Raleigh was the fact that she was so refreshingly uncomplicated for a Manhattan career woman. As he learned to know her better, and as he became aware of the way in which she had faced her personal difficulties and disappointments, his attraction for her deepened into admiration, and eventually adoration. If he had had to choose one word to describe Ivy, he would not have chosen beautiful, industrious, intelligent, charming, or loving, though she was all of these. He would have chosen wholesome.

McCoy was a man in his forties who looked like a man in his forties. His somewhat round face was neither young nor old, but pleasingly mature, and remarkably lacking in signs of dissipation or anxiety. His eyes were lustrous, with laugh lines at their corners, and his head was balding. He was average in height, and his form leaned to the heavy side, though he was not fat. McCoy believed in exercising the body as regularly as the mind, and he had just come from a swim at the University Club.

As he waited for Henry in the small elevator, a boy entered and stood beside him. McCoy glanced at him with amusement, noting the loud yellow shirt, the peg in his pants, the long yellow hair that came to a tail at the back of his head. McCoy thought of Bardo Raleigh, and how different he was from most youngsters. Sometimes his difference vaguely irritated McCoy, for while Bar and he always met each other on firm, man-to-man ground, he was unable to unbend when he was with the boy, unable to grow close to him or fond of him. He liked Bar well enough, but he often wished he were the kind of lad a fellow could take to the World Series.

When Henry ambled into the elevator, both McCoy and the boy spoke at the same time, both saying: "Five."

Henry said, "Both going to the Raleighs', huh?" in a flat, matter-of-fact voice. In all the years McCoy had been going up and down in that elevator at 1011, Henry had never once taken the floor for granted.

The boy beside McCoy said, "I'm going there, man. Can't say for him."

He didn't look at Claude until Claude said, "I'm going there too."

He glanced up at Claude then, a friendly and rather skittish smile slanting his lips. "You going to Bardo's party, man?" he asked.

"I'm going to see *Mrs.* Raleigh," McCoy answered.

"Yeah? I don't know her."

"You'll meet her." Claude grinned. He said, "My name's McCoy—Claude McCoy."

"I go by the name Flip myself," the boy said.

"Did you go to school with Bar?"

"Who, me?" Flip's face beamed with pleasure. "Naw! I mean, like I couldn't make that scene. I'm strictly local talent."

McCoy laughed then, and so did Flip.

Flip said, "Bardo, there, he's a real gray cat, you know? Like, gray matter and all. Crazy!"

"I dig it." McCoy chuckled.

"Yeah?" Flip looked at him in surprise. "You speak a little Chinese yourself, huh?"

"I'm really pretty square, man," McCoy admitted.

Johnny was late, but he walked slowly. He had kissed a girl.

He passed by the National City Bank on the corner of Ninety-first Street and Madison Avenue, and he touched the red brick with his fingers. For the first time now he felt the night around him, enveloping him, hiding him like a curtain. It was hot. It was ·a night when the lucky people sat in rooms with closed windows, air conditioners on; and a night when the unlucky people complained, perspired, drank beer or tea or lemonade, and talked of winter. It was a quiet night. The *Conquest of Everest* was playing at the Trans-lux down at Eighty-fifth. Tomorrow, rain was forecast. But tonight bare-legged women wore their sheerest summer dresses, men mopped their brows and said, "Jesus, the heat!" and yellow dogs slept panting in shop doorways.

It was the night of the second day of August in the year 1953, and Johnny knew how the breast of a young girl felt.

Inside a store along the avenue, a radio played. It was a summer when the same song was heard over and over and everywhere:

Love-bitten, smitten, smitten—
Sittin' in a daze,
Goin' through a phase . . .

A man and woman passed Johnny, and he heard the
man say to her, "Well, why didn't you wear your blue
dress? I *told* you it was a scorcher tonight."

Johnny thought, they're married. They dress and un-
dress in front of each other, and they don't even think
anything about it.

A big black tomcat sat staring sadly out of the window
of a delicatessen. Johnny thought of her black hair. Then
he thought of the whole thing over again. Why had she
made that noise when he touched her there? What did a
noise like that mean?"

One day at the store something had happened that
Johnny remembered now. A boy was waiting up by the
soda fountain for a girl he was going to walk home, but
she wasn't in any hurry. She was standing by a booth talking to these other girls. Finally the boy shouted, "Hey, beet
head. Are you *coming,* or are you just breathing hard?"
She was so mad at him she wouldn't walk with him. Johnny remembered he had remarked to Flip, "Girls are loony,
huh? Why should she get so p.o.'d just 'cause a guy calls
her 'beet head'?"

Flip had said, "That wasn't it, man." His shoulders had
shaken with laughter. "That's a good one, huh, Wyle?"

Johnny decided he'd better stop thinking about it. He
had to. He crossed Madison and went down Ninety-fourth
Street toward Fifth. Bardo Raleigh left him cold. He
wished Flip had never given Raleigh his phone number,
and he had not been asked to his party. Flip and Manny
and he could have had more fun just hanging around the
store, the way they'd done other nights. Raleigh thought
he was the Prince of Wales or something. Who *fenced,*
anyway?

Before he turned in at 1011, he saw a boy and girl
locked in an embrace on a bench across the street. Ah—
love-bitten, smitten, smitten, sittin' in a damn old daze, he
thought to himself. He walked through the door of the
apartment house laughing and snapping his fingers. But
still he couldn't stop thinking: Why did she make a noise
like that when I touched her there? What does a noise
like that mean?

8

What bound these four very different boys together was a compulsion to watch other people in agony. . . .

—From *"Kill for Thrill"* in **Real Life Crimes**

THEY HAD SPENT two and a half hours in the apartment at 1011 Fifth, and now they stood outside the building. They were restless and unsure about what to do next. They had devoured six bags of potato chips and a dozen bottles of soft drinks, and Bardo had done most of the talking. Manny had listened eagerly to him; Johnny had thought about something else, something he could not stop thinking of; and Flip had sulked. It had really hurt him more than it had made him mad when Bardo had greeted him by saying, "Your shirt is tawdry, mister. Your shirt is infinitely gawdy and tawdry and without any taste whatsoever, mister." That fellow—what was his name?—McCoy. He had taken up for Flip.

"It's O.K.," he had said. "I think it's O.K.!"

She had too, Mrs. Raleigh. She had said, "Bar, you *are* a crab tonight. Flip has a nice shirt on."

Bardo would not relent. "I found it offensive," he had answered.

They had decided to go out in a random, haphazard way, an hour or so after Mrs. Raleigh left the apartment with McCoy. Bernie's was still open, but no one suggested going there. No one suggested going anywhere. Standing idly at the curb in front of the building, they watched the star-peppered night sky and smelled the muggy August air. Flip shinned up the pole holding up the canopy, let his feet dangle a moment, and dropped back to the asphalt. Johnny traced the crack in the sidewalk with the toe of his shoe and whistled an aimless tune through his teeth. Manny sank his hands into the pockets of his trousers and stared vacantly at the faces of the passengers riding the Fifth Avenue bus up to Washington Heights.

When Bardo began walking, the three straggled along with him, like dogs roving in the night, looking for nothing special, wandering around. Manny caught up with Bardo and walked beside him. Flip and Johnny strolled listlessly behind.

"He's a crazy cat, huh, Wyle?" Flip said. "Like, what he said about my shirt."

"Uh-huh," Johnny answered. The funny thing about a girl's body was that it was full of soft, strange, secret places.

"I never had anyone say things like that to me. You know?"

"He's a jerk."

"It's crazy in a way. I mean, I don't mind him. Even when he sounds off like he did, all about gawdy and tawdy and all that. He's got class, you know? Like he calls his old lady by her first name. Me, I'd get my head bashed in."

"She's not so old," Johnny said. "She's got a swell figure."

"He's educated. You go to old Yale-jail, you meet up with a million guys like that, I bet."

"I'm not going to college," Johnny said. "I might just get a job and get married or something dumb like that." Christ! To take your clothes off in front of a girl and not think anything about it. Day in and day out. It was queer to imagine it.

"Who needs college, anyway?" Flip snorted. "I seen a lot of them Joe Colleges come into the place and think they're hot. Make with the big-deal line. 'Lookit the beer mugs.' " Flip raised his voice and imitated the high, squealing voices of the girls who came with them. "And 'Lookit the little bandstand. What a cute place.' Jeez, I mean, why don't they say something in college if it's such a big-deal language?"

Johnny said, "I was up on the roof with this screwy girl tonight and—"

"Oh, Christ in a big square bucket!" Flip interrupted him abruptly. "I forgot to get my goddamn hair cut." He drew a finger across his throat. He said, "Curtains!"

Then they were all standing together on the corner of Ninety-sixth Street and Fifth Avenue, waiting for the light to change.

When it did, they walked across the street, and Bardo

pointed toward a small park surrounded by bushes and a black iron gate that stood open. "As a youngster," he announced, "I played in this area."

Manny said, "Gee, so did I, Bardo. Me and my brother used to seesaw here. That's funny, isn't it?"

"I wouldn't say so," Bardo answered.

"I mean, it's a coincidence, Bardo."

"Yes, it is, mister," Bardo agreed.

"I bet Johnny did, too," Manny said enthusiastically. Over his shoulder he asked Johnny, "Did you, Wyle?"

"Some," Johnny said. No bells had rung when he kissed her; no dizziness, nothing. Just surprise. And he liked it. And then *that* happened. On television, when those good-looking guys got in a clinch with those long-haired, chesty dolls that wore the slits up their skirts in smoky night clubs, did it happen to them too? Was there some way a guy could stop it?

They were entering the small park now.

Flip said, "I'm going to have a swing," and he sauntered over to the swings set in a row between two poles. The chains creaked as he sat down. He sang, "*Oh, he flies through the air with the craziest ease, the daring young cat on the flying trapeze.*"

Johnny reached down and picked up a handful of sand from the sandpile, sifting it through his hands. Bardo stood on one side of him and Manny sat down on a bench. Flip was singing at the top of his lungs, making the swing go higher and higher.

"You're rather reticent this evening, Wylie," Bardo commented. "Problems?"

"No," Johnny said. "I don't know."

"We ought to pep you up, mister. You're in the dumps."

Johnny shrugged. "It's hot, I guess."

"We all need pepping up," Bardo said. "Except Herr Heine."

"Better not call him that to his face."

"Herr Heine? Why not?"

"He doesn't like stuff like that. German stuff. He gets sore."

"Now, I don't know why he should," Bardo said.

"At school once a guy called him Hitler, and Flip darn near killed him. I never saw him so mad."

"He should have been proud," Bardo said. "Hitler was a great, great man."

"The Jews didn't think so."

"You believe that propaganda about Hitler picking on the Jews, mister? You believe that archaic theory? Hitler was above that. Hitler had nothing *whatsoever* to do with who was responsible for that little game. Herr Hermann Göring, fortune-hunting husband of an epileptic! Married for money; then *ran around*. Herr Hermann Göring, a whoremonger who gave Roehm a blood bath because Roehm was unfortunate enough to be a homosexual. Göring, mister. Göring is your man. Not Adolf Hitler."

Johnny said, "I don't know about those things."

"Hitler was a soldier and a gentleman!"

"O.K." Johnny said. "O.K. Cripes, don't get so excited!"

"You ought to get your facts straight about Der Führer before you make erroneous innuendoes, Wylie. A man who's going to be a lawyer ought to be very careful to get his facts straight."

"I'm going to be a soda jerk," Johnny said, "so I don't have to."

Flip leaped from the swing then, leaving the wooden seat to snap in the air and bang back against the iron pole, twisting the chain so that it spun and rattled. He landed in the sand at Manny's feet. "Look, Ma, I'm dancing!" he chortled. Manny grinned down at him. Flip stood up and spanked the dirt off his trousers, then ruffled Manny's hair playfully. "You old snake charmer, you!"

Manny said, "Did you ever hear of such a thing as a herpetologist, Flip?"

"I hear you talking but you can't come in," Flip answered airily, and he turned and called to the others, "Let's mosey along. The night is young and we're so beauti-ful!"

Again the four started walking in the capricious attitude that dominated the evening. Flip's spirits were improved; he was amused now, and Manny had grown contentedly quiet. Bardo snapped his fingers in a persistent marching rhythm, and shuffled his feet until he was in step with Wylie. Johnny pulled a twig from a bush he passed, stuck it between his teeth, and alternately bit and sucked on it. They went out of the park and up on the path between the stone wall along Fifth Avenue and the road separating them from the reservoir. Cabs sped past them, and except for the headlights of the fleeting taxis and the few widely spaced street lights, the way was not brightly lit. At intervals, ahead of them, there were benches.

"The police exercise their horses over there." Manny pointed toward the bridle path that circled the reservoir. "I was going to be one once."

Flip jumped up on an empty bench. "A horse?" he said. He spread his hands above his head and did a mock jackknife dive to the ground.

Manny said seriously, "No, a policeman."

"They ought to get less exercise for their horses and more for themselves," Bardo said. "This area is infested with loiterers."

Flip picked up a stick and banged the tree trunks as they moved along.

Johnny saw the pair first. They were almost hidden from view, on a bench pushed off to the side of the lane, facing the four. They were a boy and girl, lying down on the bench. His white shirt showed in the glimmer of light, and a gold charm bracelet on her bare arm, which was wrapped around his shirt, sparkled in speckled darts of illumination.

Johnny whispered, "Hey, lookit! Lovers."

"Man, oh, man!" Flip giggled. "They're really going to town."

"Golly!" Manny said. "Sweethearts."

They all stopped and watched, and Bardo snapped, "Dis-gusting! That guy must think he's some kind of a wise guy. Bringing a girl here!"

"Anything could happen," Manny said.

"Yeah, like it *is* happening!"

"Let's sneak up on them," Johnny said. "Let's watch them."

"Let's scare hell out of them!" Flip said. "Let's sneak up and give 'em the old spook scene!"

"No, let's *watch*," Johnny said.

Bardo's curt tone cut into the conversation. "We'll approach them directly, like *men!*" he announced. "Come on!"

He led them, marching ahead of them, while Flip and Johnny followed like obedient sheep, and Manny shuffled behind without much confidence. When Bardo reached the bench he commanded the startled boy, "Pop to, mister! On the double!"

"Huh?" The boy sat up, bewildered. His hand fumbled

to button his shirt, which was half open at his chest. His black curly hair was tossed and wild-looking. His dark eyes blinked up at Bardo confusedly.

"Never mind that." Bardo slapped the boy's hand away from his shirt. "On your feet, green-belly!"

The boy stood up. He was taller than Bardo, but not really tall. He wore blue jeans with his white shirt, and moccasins on his feet. His face was lean and bony, like his body, and he had a Latin look and a slight accent. He mumbled, "I don't have no money. I'll give you what I got. Forty cents." He started to reach into his pocket, fumbling nervously.

Johnny stared at the girl. She was fixing her blouse. Her face was white and frightened, and she looked very small, but built well and rounded. Her dark hair was piled on top of her head and held in place by a cheap rhinetstone clip shaped like a wishbone. She wore a flimsy peasant blouse through which her pink bra and slip could be seen, a multicolored cotton skirt, and scuffed loafers on her bare feet.

She pleaded, "Don't hurt us. We didn't do anything."

Johnny said, "We aren't going to hurt you."

The boy was trembling as he searched his pockets. Bardo barked, "We don't want your filthy money, mister."

"Thinks we're pirates." Flip laughed. " 'At's good. The Central Park Pirates."

Manny snickered too, unenthusiastically.

"Then what do you want? What do you want?" The boy's voice became more desperate.

"What's your name, mister?"

"Carlos. Carlos Rodriguez." He was shaking. The girl sat behind him, her hands folded tightly in her lap, her wide, wet lips quivering.

"Carlos, let me ask you a question. Why did you bring this young lady here? Will you answer that?"

"Yeah, man," Flip put in. "Like, what do you think this is, a hotel or something? This ain't a hotel. This here's a park."

"We walked here," the boy answered.

"I don't think you understand, Carlos. Why did you bring her here? For what purpose?"

Johnny said to the girl, "You don't have to be scared of us."

"Naw," Manny said.

The boy trembled. "I—I brought her here to— smooch."

"To smooch," Bardo said disgustedly. "To *smooch*."

"Man, like I think you was intent on more than smooching with this dame, Carlos."

"My colleague is right," Bardo said.

"What's the matter?" the boy said. "What's the matter?"

The girl whined, "Don't hurt us. We didn't do anything."

"The matter, mister," Bardo said, "is that you intended to molest this girl, mister. You brought this girl here to molest her."

"Cripes, Bardo!" Johnny turned his back on the girl and picked at a piece of bark on a scrawny young tree beside the bench. Manny listened to Bardo without moving or looking at the girl any more.

"It's against the law, mister," Bardo said. "You can go to prison for that."

"Man, like, he ought to have some discipline," Flip said.

"You are one hundred per cent correct, Herr Heine."

Johnny shot a quick look at Flip to see his reaction, but he saw only a smile and bright, self-assured eyes. Maybe he had not heard.

"Leave him alone!" the girl suddenly shouted, jumping to her feet. She punched Flip's leg with her fist. "Leave Carlos alone! Bully!"

"No," the boy told her, trying to push her back with his nervous hands. "No, Linda. No."

Bardo put his arms behind his back, clasping his hands there, standing very erect. "Linda," he said coldly, "I want to know something."

"Bully! Bully!" she shouted at him.

Flip grabbed her by the arm and held her tightly, hurting her. "Watch your crazy tongue!" he said. "You want it cut out of you?" He reached into his pocket.

"I want to know something," Bardo persisted. "I want you to tell me something, Linda."

"You're hurting me," she said to Flip. He had something in his hand that was ebony-colored and shining in the dim light.

"I want to know if you came here with Carlos this evening to smooch."

"Sure. Sure. We came together. There a law? Oww, Jesus," she whined. "My arm!"

Johnny whirled around and started to say something;
then he saw the knife Flip held, the blade clean and brilliant. Flip held it right under her left breast, which pouted
impudently through the sheer blouse. Johnny just watched
then, the same way Manny did, with surprise and wonder
too great to permit concern.

"You shout, you scream," Flip warned, "you get this—
pronto!"

"Oh, God, God," the boy moaned. His whole body was
wet with sweat now, and his knees were rubbery. The girl
cried.

Manny spoke softly. "Where did you get the knife,
Flip?"

"You brought this girl here to rape her, is that it, mister?" Bardo walked over to Carlos and leered up at him.
"Is that why you brought her here?"

"No, no. God help me. No." The boy was crying too
now.

"No, he didn't," the girl sobbed. "No, he didn't."

"How'd your shirt get unbuttoned, mister?"

Carlos' fingers shook as he felt for the buttons; tears
streamed down his face. "I—I—"

"Like, little Linda here did it, huh, man?"

"Leave us alone," the girl begged. "Oh, please, please.
My mother's sick."

"She'd be sick if she knew where *you* were," Bardo said.
"She'd be sick if she knew you were lying on a bench in
a park letting a young buck maul your whole body. Your
mother's sick! Why aren't you home with your mother?"

"She's waiting for me," the girl cried.

Flip still held her arm, the knife in his hand. Manny
was frowning, hanging behind Bardo, and Johnny was
frozen to the spot near the tree.

"How'd your blouse get disheveled, Miss Linda?" Bardo
said. "It *was* disheveled, was it not?"

The girl couldn't talk.

Flip said, "Half off her. He was feeling her."

"Is that the most interesting thing you can think to do
with your leisure, mister?"

Carlos only whimpered.

"Is that what your shallow mind invents for your diver-
sion?"

Flip hooted. "Man, oh, man, how you carry on!" He
grinned at Bardo with admiration.

Bardo said, "Herr Heine, we're going to discipline these two juvenile delinquents. Herr Heine, I put the method of discipline for the female member of this duet in your capable hands. My experience has not been along those lines."

The girl began to cry hysterically. Flip jerked her to him. "Shut up!" he said. "Shut your yap!"

Manny said, "She's afraid, that's all, Flip." His voice sounded far off in the distance.

"Want to kiss her, Wylie?" Flip asked Johnny.

Johnny had a funny look in his eyes, as though he were hypnotized. He couldn't say any words; he just shook his head. He was standing by the tree.

"Ladies first," Bardo said. "Deal out the punishment, mister."

"Yeah." Flip scratched his head. "Like, what'll it be? Got to think this one over."

The boy stood cowering before Bardo, his nose running, his face streaked with tears. "Her mother's got asthma," he murmured.

"Is that any reason for you to molest her, mister? Is that any reason for you to try to remove her blouse and look at her, mister? That's what you were doing. She was looking at you and you were looking at her."

"No," the boy blubbered. "No, no."

Flip squared his shoulders in a decisive gesture. He said, "That's right. You want to see her and she wants you to, huh? That's right. That's the way it was." He turned to the girl, still gripping her by the wrist, his knife in his other hand. "Sure," he said. "That's the way it was. All reet! I dig it now." He stood back from her, letting go of her wrist, but pointing his knife at her as he directed, "O.K., Lady Godiva, take off the blouse."

She stood motionless, unable to answer or to move.

"Go ahead," Flip said. "Nothing's going to happen to you. I'm just giving you your wish. Like I'm your fairy godfather." His voice grew more terse when she still did not move. "Unbutton that piece of nothing and take it off," he said.

The boy's shoulders slumped and he began to groan, his head down, his hands rubbing his face. "Brace, mister!" Bardo shouted. He put a fist in the boy's gut, and the boy sank to his knees in the dirt, weeping helplessly. Bardo said, "O.K., green-belly, stay there. Your turn comes next."

Dazedly the girl undid the buttons of her blouse. Flip reached and yanked it off her shoulders. He rolled it into a ball and held it in his hand. She stood there quivering, her pink slip plain and worn. Behind them, Manny began to cough. Johnny was rooted to the spot where he stood watching. Bardo watched the scene disinterestedly, the boy crumpled at his feet.

"Let the straps down," Flip said to the girl.

"Please. Please. I only want—"

"Do what I tell you," Flip said. He held the knife menacingly. The boy began to pray softly in Spanish.

She raised trembling fingers to her bare shoulders and slipped the straps over them; the top of her slip, and her bra, fell to her waist. She wailed, "Please. Please."

Flip laughed, looking at her. "Now your boy friend don't have to do it, 'cause there you are. Ain't that pretty, now? Ain't you just too pretty for words, now?"

Manny said, "Let her go, Flip. You ought to let her go now." He looked once at the girl and then away.

"I ain't going to *touch* her, man."

"You ought to be ashamed of yourself," Bardo said to the girl. "You ought to be filled with shame for what a sight you are! Half naked! Half naked in a park!" He jerked the boy by the shoulder. "Is this the dirty thing you came here for, mister? To do this to this girl?"

"Pity us," the boy wailed. "Think of God."

"I pity you!" Bardo said. "You'll never know how I pity you, mister."

The girl just stood there, tears brimming from closed eyes, her head down, trying to cover herself with her hands, but unable to.

"Want to pinch her, Wyle?" Flip giggled at Johnny over his shoulder. "Come on, Wyle. Here she is!"

Johnny had never seen a girl this way before. Until that evening, he had never touched one. He could not stop staring. He could not stop thinking with a flood of amazement that a girl looked so *different*. He had seen statues, and photographs of girls, but it simply was not the same as this.

"Come on, Wyle," Flip urged. "Pinch 'em."

Manny said, "You could hurt someone with that knife, Flip."

"Relax, Pollack." Bardo looked over his shoulder at Manny.

The boy on his knees prayed plaintively, "Merciful God in heaven, see our misery."

Manny said, "I'm relaxed, but—"

"What are you worried about, Pollack? We're just teaching these two juvenile delinquents a lesson. Don't you understand that, mister?"

"Yes," Manny answered. "I understand that."

Flip said again, "Come on, Wyle. You afraid, John boy?"

Johnny moved away from the tree and came slowly forward. The girl shrank back as he approached her. "Put your hands at your sides!" Flip yelled. "You hear me?" The girl obeyed, and Johnny came closer. He stood looking at her. Her body was shaking with the sobs inside of her.

"Go on, Wyle. That a boy!" Flip slapped his knee with his hand and chuckled. Bardo stood watching apathetically, his lip curled in revulsion.

Johnny put his hand out, and the girl shrank back again.

"Please," she said. "Please don't." Tears ran down her face and dropped to her bare flesh.

"I'm not going to hurt you," Johnny said solemnly.

"Don't hurt me."

"I'm not going to," Johnny said. His speech was thick and husky.

"Get it over with!" Bardo said impatiently.

Very slowly Johnny brought his fingers to her and touched her breast. His palm flattened on her there, and then as though he had felt a burning coal, he jerked his hand away.

"Big thrill, huh?" Flip said. He had suddenly lost interest in the girl, and he turned away from her, looking back at Manny. "What you doing, Manny?"

Johnny said to the girl, "I didn't hurt you. I said I wouldn't."

"Leave me alone," the girl wept. "Let me go home. My mother's sick."

Manny answered Flip, "Nothing. Just standing here."

"Pollack has dignity!" Bardo said. "Don't you, Pollack?"

"I don't know, Bardo."

"But *you* have no dignity, mister." Bardo poked the boy at his feet with his shoe. Flip watched Bardo and so did

Manny. Johnny stood away from the girl, but facing her. He said, "I'm sorry about your mother. . . ." His voice trailed off. He didn't look at her any more. He looked at the ground.

"Let me go home," she said. "Please. Please. Can't I go home."

"On your feet, Carlos!" Bardo said.

Johnny touched Flip's shoulder. "She wants to go home," he said. "Let her go home."

Carlos struggled to his feet, while Bardo reached into his back pocket.

Manny said, "She needs her blouse."

The girl was pulling her straps back up, the knuckles of her hands rubbing her wet eyes.

"Let her go home, why don't you, Flip?" Johnny said. "Give her her blouse."

"This is going to be short, sweet, and simple," Bardo said.

Flip stared with fascination at the ring Raleigh held in his hand. He tossed the balled-up blouse at Johnny indifferently. Johnny took it and shook it out. He handed it to the girl, who snatched it from him. "Here's your blouse," he said. "It's just wrinkled a little."

The girl began to run. Johnny watched her go.

"Grab your ankles, mister," Bardo directed the boy. "Bend over and grab your ankles with your hands." The boy did as he was told.

Bardo took the ring and placed it on a handkerchief on the ground between the boy's spread legs. He said, "Bend and squat, mister, and kiss that ring!"

The boy tried, but he was crying. He lost his grip on his ankles.

"Keep ahold of those ankles, green-belly," Bardo shouted. "Kiss that ring!"

Grunting, weeping, the boy bent, straining his thin bones, the blood rushing to his face, until gradually and at last his lips touched the gold ring. Then Bardo, behind him, drew his foot back violently and kicked the boy in the groin, sending him sprawling forward, his face buried in the dirt. The boy's screams of pain rent the still air of the summer night. He lay with his face in the dust, blood trickling from his nose.

Manny sucked in his breath and gaped at the figure lying there.

Flip said, "Man, you really dish it out!"

Johnny said, "Christ, Bardo! Christ!"

Bardo bent over and picked up the ring and the hand-kerchief. He put them back in his pocket.

"Come on," he said tiredly.

He began to walk away, and Flip went with him. Manny still stared at the boy, who was lifting his face now, moving his legs.

"You—hurt?" Manny said.

"He kicked him too goddamn hard," Johnny said.

Bardo yelled, "Come on, you two! He's got a nosebleed, that's all."

Side by side, Johnny and Manny stood for a moment more looking down at Carlos. The boy was getting to his knees, his face bloody and striped with tear lines. He said, "God in heaven, leave me alone. Oh, my God, my God."

"Come on," Johnny said. "He doesn't want us around gaping at him."

Manny followed Johnny, looking once and then again over his shoulder at the boy. Then he looked straight ahead, the same way Johnny did, and neither of them said anything for a long time. They could hear Bardo's and Flip's voices ahead of them, and the sound of the cabs whizzing by, the way they had been doing the whole time while the four of them were off in the shadows by the bench with the boy and girl. At the end of the walk, up where the lane swerved closer to the reservoir, they could feel the slight breeze from the water and see the pumpkin moon through the trees. They turned out of the park at Ninety-first Street, going on to Fifth Avenue again. The street lights were bright. A man passed them walking a bulldog.

Johnny was the first to speak. He said, "I might as well go on home. It's eleven-thirty."

"Maybe I ought to, too," Manny said. "What are they going to do?"

Bardo and Flip were standing on the sidewalk, midway between Ninety-first and Ninety-second, waiting for Manny and Johnny to catch up.

"I don't know," Johnny said dully. "I'm going home."

"That was sure something, wasn't it?" Manny said, looking down to see the expression on Johnny's face.

There was no particular expression there. He said, "Yeah."

From somewhere off back in the bushes behind the
stone wall along Fifth, a cricket chirped. Flip called,
"Hurry up, you guys."

Manny said, "Supposed to rain tomorrow. Sky doesn't
look like it."

"She was scared stiff," Johnny said.

Manny said, "She thought we were going to hurt her."

When they reached Bardo and Flip, Flip still held the
knife in his hand, the blade snapped inside of the handle
now.

"They're outlawed, I think," Manny said, looking at it.

They stood there in a group on the sidewalk.

Bardo said, "Yes, mister, they are. You ought to put it
away before someone gets hurt."

Flip tossed it in the air, caught it with one hand, and
jammed it into his pocket. He said, "Boy, am I going to
catch hell when I get home!"

"Why?" Manny said.

"I just am."

Johnny sighed wearily. "I got to beat it." He looked at
Flip. "Going my way?"

"Might as well," Flip said.

"You go *my* way, don't you, Pollack?" Bardo asked.

"Yes. I cut over Ninety-fourth."

They stood there a moment, looking idly around them,
at the cars waiting for the light at Ninety-first Street, at
the two doormen lounging at the entrance of the apartment building on the corner, and at the dog-walkers going
along the grass near the wall on their side of the avenue.
Flip stretched and yawned noisily, and Johnny socked the
palm of his hand with his fist in a persistent, offhand manner. Manny was pulling a loose button from the jacket of
his summer suit, and Bardo was rolling up the sleeves of
his shirt.

Finally Bardo said, "Well, gentlemen, let's call it a
night."

"It was kicks," Flip said.

"We ought to get together next week. You gentlemen
free?"

Flip said, "If I'm living, man."

Johnny didn't say anything, and Manny said he guessed
he would be.

"We'll keep in touch during the week," Bardo said. "We
ought to keep in touch."

"Crazy!"

"If you call me and I'm not home, you can always leave a message," Manny said.

Flip clapped his hands across Johnny's shoulders. " 'Mon, Wyle, boy," he said. "Let's cut out. Christ, am I going to catch hell!"

"So long," Johnny said.

The pair turned and went down Fifth toward Ninety-first Street.

Manny and Raleigh went silently along, Raleigh humming "March of the Men of Harlech," Manny playing with the button he had got off his suit. Once Manny said, "I hope that boy's all right. Not hurt or anything."

"He's all right, mister," Raleigh said. He kept on humming the march.

At the corner of Ninety-fourth Street, Bardo shook Manny's hand.

"I'd like to see this remarkable snake of yours sometime, Pollack."

"No kidding?" Manny said.

"No kidding, mister. Bring him around sometime." Bardo saluted Manny. "Good night Mister."

Manny started to go, and then he stopped. He said, "Bardo?"

Turning, Bardo looked back at him.

"Thanks," Manny said. "Thanks for the party."

"You've got manners, Pollack. That's what Bardo Raleigh likes about you. You're a gentleman!"

Manny beamed. The two boys waved then, and went off in opposite directions.

"They were a strange assortment, all right," Claude McCoy told Ivy Raleigh over brandy at Maria's.

"I know," she said. "I was surprised. Bar never fails to amaze me."

"How do you mean?"

"Oh, you know. He's sort of chameleon-like, the way he adapts himself to any environment."

"He doesn't really change, though. I think the environment adapts itself to Bar."

Ivy laughed. "If *he* has anything to say about it, I guess. That poor boy with that awful shirt. I was mortified for him!"

"The hipster. Yes."

"And then that terribly sullen youngster—the one with the mustache. He gave me an eerie feeling."

"He had the weight of the world on his shoulders."

"The other one—Emanuel, I think his name was. He was pleasant."

"I wonder what they're doing now. What do four completely opposite kids do when they get together?"

"Oh, they drink Cokes and tell naughty stories, I suppose."

Claude imitated Bardo's voice. "Cokes rot your teeth, mister."

They laughed together then.

Ivy said, "Poor Bar. I hope he has enough to occupy his mind this summer."

"They were a strange assortment, all right," McCoy repeated. He took a swallow of his brandy. "Hey," he said, reaching across for Ivy Raleigh's hand. "Let's forget the younger generation for a while, huh, and talk about something serious?"

"Let's," Ivy said.

9

"Remember once," Manny said, "couple years ago. Mom and me and Irv were playing Monopoly. Mom had hotels set up on both the Boardwalk and Park, and Irv controlled the whole row after 'Go.' When I shook the dice I didn't throw them right away. I guess I just knew when they landed I'd probably be out of the game. So I held them in my hand. Mom said, 'You're so slow, Emanuel! It isn't any fun to play with a poke!' You know what Irv said?" He looked up at Dr. Mannerheim, a faint smile at the corners of his lips.

"What did he say?" she asked.

"Irv said, 'Some people move fast, and some move slow. Not everyone's like everyone else, Mom.' That was what he said." Manny looked down at his hands. He said, "He was a swell guy. He could do and say anything just right."

It was Tuesday, the fifth of August, and Manny was having his second session with the psychologist. He would go twice a week now, Tuesdays and Saturdays. Because the clinic down on Eighteenth Street was undergoing remodeling, Dr. Mannerheim saw him in her spacious apartment on Central Park West. They sat in the large gray-walled front room, where the low row of windows looked out over the trees of the park, and beyond, in the distance, at the boxed-in buildings of the East side in the Eighties. Manny sat on the edge of the blue studio couch. Dr. Mannerheim faced him across a small square coffee table, her black woven-tape chair pulled to one side.

There was a pause while Manny cleaned the dirt from under his nails with the nail of his thumb. Dr. Mannerheim lit a cigarette, crossed her legs, and said, "Tell me about Sincere, Emanuel."

70

She was an averaged-sized, attractive woman in her early forties. Her short brown hair, curling loosely, framed a pleasant oval-shaped face dominated by keen, alert light-blue eyes. As she smoked she watched Manny, leaning forward occasionally to drop an ash into a round piece of gray pottery that lay on the table between them. Once Manny pushed the ash tray closer to her, then pulled it back to its original position, saying, "I guess it belongs in the center. I don't smoke. I know guys my age who do, though."

Now he said, "Sincere has a black tongue. Some snakes have red tongues, or green ones, or even black-and-red ones, or yellow. Depends." He frowned and picked at a hangnail. "I think that's what scares my mother about him. He flicks it in and out all the time." Manny imitated the motion with his own tongue. Then he blushed and sank back into the cushions of the couch. Apologetically he added, "All snakes do it."

"Do you know why?" Dr. Mannerheim asked. Her voice was interested.

"Sure." His face brightened and he sat up again. "For touching things some," he said, "but mostly to tell what's going on. If I move, and I'm around Sinny's cage, he can tell because he can feel the breeze I make with his tongue. If he was on his own, see, he'd use his tongue to find food, or to get out of the way of trouble."

"You know quite a bit about snakes, don't you, Emanuel?"

"Sure. I mean, yes, I do. Maybe I ought to be a herpetologist when I grow up."

"Maybe so."

"Do you think that's what I ought to be? A herpetologist?"

"What do you think?"

Manny shrugged. He said, "Do you know what one is? It's someone who's an *authority* on snakes."

"Yes, I know."

"Snakes don't hurt people. Most of them don't," Manny said after a moment. "But people think they do. I mean, some people don't even give a snake a chance to prove himself. What's he supposed to do? He's not *like* people. I mean, he doesn't eat with a knife and fork." Manny licked the place on his thumb where he had ripped off the hangnail. He said, "My mother thinks Sincere is mean the way he eats. All snakes swallow their food whole. Did you know that?"

"No," Dr. Mannerheim admitted, "I didn't."

Manny said, "It's funny." He snickered and sat on his hands. "I'm telling you things."

"Why is that funny?"

"You're supposed to tell *me*."

"Tell you what, Emanuel?"

"What to do," he said. "Aren't you?"

"No." She smiled.

"Bardo, this friend of mine," Manny said, "thinks I'd be a swell herpetologist. He wants to see my snake."

"He's the one whose party you attended last week, isn't he?"

"It was just a get-together," Manny answered.

"And how was it?"

"We went for a walk up by the reservoir. Do you know that path?"

"I think so."

"It's dark, and the cabs just whiz by without paying any attention. Anything could happen."

"And did anything happen?"

"We saw some sweethearts up there on a bench. They shouldn't have been there."

"And what did you do when you saw them?"

"Nothing." Manny shrugged. "We just warned them they ought not to be up there in the dark."

"And what did they say?"

"They went home, I guess. This girl's mother was sick. Her mother had asthma."

"Did she tell you that?"

"Yeah." Manny nodded. "And Bardo said if her mother was sick, she should have been home. That was right, wasn't it?"

"What do you think?"

"Of course!" Manny said emphatically. "Her mother had asthma!" He brought a hand out from under him and scratched his ear. "Once," he said, "*my* mother was sick. She had some bug that was going around. Irv got up early and fixed her breakfast—scrambled eggs and everything— and he put it all on a tray and served it to her right in bed. I mean, he put Worcestershire sauce and everything in them. He used to know things like that. He was a swell guy."

"He must have been."

"Worcestershire sauce is good in scrambled eggs," Manny said. "Did you ever try it?"

Dr. Mannerheim agreed, "Yes, it's very good." She waited some seconds to see if Pollack would add anything to this, and then, glancing at her watch, she said, "Well, Emanuel, I guess that's all for now."

"We just talk, don't we?" Manny said, getting up from the couch.

The doctor rose too, walking with him down the hallway toward the door. "Did you think we'd do something else?"

"You're supposed to tutor me or something, I thought," Manny said. "I don't know."

"It's more fun just to talk, isn't it, Emanuel?" She smiled as she opened the door.

"Sure," Manny said. "I mean yes, it is. I don't need a boss."

Outside, the noon sun was boiling. Manny decided to cut through the park on his way home. That afternoon his mother was taking him to see *The Las Vegas Story*, which was playing over at the Grande on Eighty-sixth Street. Whenever a movie with Victor Mature was showing, his mother went to see it. She said he reminded her, in a way, of Irving. "Around the eyes," she said, "but your brother wasn't conceited. I can tell that Victor Mature is. Irving was always nice to everyone."

"How do you know Victor Mature is conceited?" Manny's father had asked.

"Oh, God, Nat—there you go! Picking on everything I say."

"You shouldn't say things unless you know for sure they're true," his father had answered. "People have enough trouble in this world."

That noon the world to Manny seemed remarkably without trouble. The sky was blue and cloudless, and though it was sweltering, the park gave the illusion of coolness and calm. Solitary figures sat on the benches in the shade, reading, eating their lunches, watching the small children run up and down the grassy knolls, and dozing. A young man sitting on a rock atop one of the knolls pounded the keys of a portable typewriter that was balanced on his knees.

Manny walked along humming to himself and thinking

vaguely of Dr. Mannerheim. He decided that perhaps his
father had been right after all about psychologists. She
had not told him anything important or wise; in fact, she
had not said very much the whole hour. Manny had had
to keep the conversation going. Maybe she was bashful,
he speculated; maybe it was hard for her to warm up to
people. Manny knew what *that* was like. Three years ago,
at his *bar mizvah,* when his mother and father had held
that party for him in the apartment, Manny had sat off in
a corner playing with the new gold pen and pencil set he
had received, while everyone around him laughed and
talked. "Come on, Manski," his brother had teased him
playfully. "Circulate, fellow. Today you are a man!"

"I don't know anyone here very well," Manny had said.

"Well, get to know them. They won't bite, Manski."

"I know they won't," Manny had answered solemnly,
but still he remained apart. His best friends—his only real
friends, Flip and Wylie, had not been present. He could
have talked to them because he knew them so well. He
knew them better than anyone else.

Manny stopped when he passed a rock, and bent over
to look under it. Wherever he went he carried a glass tube
with a cork top, for catching bugs. He kept it in his pants
pocket, and that noon he already had two prisoners: a
cockroach he had spotted on the stairway of his apartment
building and a grasshopper he had picked off a bush. There
was nothing under the rock but an angleworm and some
red ants. Sincere didn't eat either worms or ants, so Manny kicked the rock back with his foot and kept on going.

The sun had a slow, insidious, fatiguing effect, so that
Manny did not realize he was tired until he reached the
top of a hill overlooking a pond. He sat down in a clump
of grass, mopped his brow with a handkerchief, and peered
under two more rocks he could reach from where he sat.
He thought of strolling down toward the park zoo to see
the snakes, and he thought of how cool it would be that
afternoon in the air-conditioned theater, and he thought
of how he had not told Dr. Mannerheim everything that
had happened in the park the other night. Why should
he? She hadn't asked. He leaned back as he thought these
things, until his head rested there in the dry grass, and he
watched the sky and the birds sailing in it, and he wondered if Victor Mature really was conceited, and he fell
asleep.

When he awakened there was someone sitting beside him. It startled him at first, but when he saw the pleasant expression on the man's face, he sat up and said, "I was sleeping."

"I know you were," the man said. He was middle-aged and very thin; his face was sunburned, and he wore rimless glasses and a light-gray suit, the jacket of which he carried over his arm. His tie was loosened at the collar of his white shirt, and in his short, square hands he carried a straw hat.

Manny said, "I just fell asleep."

"It's quiet here," the man said. "It's a good place to sleep."

His eyes were steady on Manny. He smiled with his lips closed. "Do you come here often?" he asked.

"I was on my way home," Manny said.

"Do you live far?"

"Just across the park. Ninety-fourth Street."

"That's a coincidence," the man said. "I'm going that way myself. I have a car. I just got out for a breath of air and to stretch my legs. My car's right down there." He pointed to an area behind him where there was a space for parking.

"Do you live near me?" Manny asked.

"I'm a salesman. I travel a lot. I'm just going your way."

"That must be nice. Be a salesman."

"It's hard work," the man said. He touched Manny's trousers. "I sell suits," he said.

"This is a suit, only I'm just wearing the pants. I lost the button off my coat. It was my brother's suit."

"You should have a suit of your own," the man said, gravely.

"I don't mind. My brother's dead. He got killed in Korea."

"I'm sorry about that, son."

"Thanks. He didn't wear this much at all. It was practically bran'-new."

"Say," the man said, "as long as we're heading in the same direction, why don't I drop you? My car's right down there."

"You don't have to. I mean, it's a lot of trouble."

"No, no—I want to. It's no trouble."

"I don't know," Manny said.

"Come on. It's too hot to walk. You'll get sunstroke."

The man stood up, and Manny did too. "I always walk in the sun," Manny said. "I don't even wear a cap. It doesn't bother me."

"Come on." The man smiled. "My car's right·down there."

They jogged down the hill and walked slowly across the field to the parking spot. The man said Manny ought to wear brown because his eyes were brown, and Manny told him the first suit he had ever had was a brown gabardine, and he had fallen off his bike and ripped the knees almost the second day he wore it. That was too bad, the man said, because brown was his color, all right. Manny said his father had taken it to a tailor and you could hardly see the patch, but he didn't wear it for good any more, because the pants were too short now.

The door of the car was open, and inside it was hot. It was parked away from the other cars, off under a tree, in the shade. The back seat was filled with boxes, and there was a melted candy bar on the front seat. When the man slid into the driver's seat, he did not lean forward to turn the key in the ignition. He put one arm over the back of the seat and sat sideways, facing Manny.

"You look like a nice kid," he said.

"Thanks."

"Do you have a lot of girl friends?"

"Uh-uh." Manny grinned, embarrassed. "I mean, no. I'm just a kid."

"How old are you?"

"Sixteen."

"That's old enough."

"I've been to dances," Manny said, "but I don't know how to dance."

The man laughed. "Too young to tango, hmm?"

"I just never learned," Manny said.

"You know, son, I might just have a suit back there that would fit you."

"I'm still growing," Manny said. "My mother says there's no sense spending money on a whole new suit until I have my growth."

"These are samples. They don't cost anything."

"How come?"

"They're mine. They're samples." The man leaned over and fingered Manny's belt. "Let's see—you'd be about a twelve, hmmm?" His hand rested on Manny's hip. "How would you like a new suit?" he said, smiling. And suddenly Manny knew what the man wanted.

When the man stopped the car at Ninety-fourth Street and Madison Avenue, Manny sat like a dummy before he saw where he was.

The man said, "I couldn't help it, kid. Do you believe that? I feel like hell. I didn't know it would throw you for such a loop, kid," the man said. "I don't know what's wrong with me."

Manny put his hand on the chromium handle of the car door. He pressed it down. He remembered that someone a long time ago had said, "Homosexuals can't help the way they are. They're born that way, mister."

The man reached over and closed the door after Manny had got out of the car. He said, "Be careful crossing the street, kid." For a moment he leaned against the open window of the automobile, watching the boy, his eyes behind his rimless glasses pained and fatuous.

Manny stood on the corner waiting for the light. He didn't look back to where the car was parked, with its motor running, at the curb. From his pocket he took out the glass tube, fondled it in his hand as he waited for the green light, and tried to remember something else he had once heard: "Contempt breeds familiarity." Was that it? What did it mean?

"It's dark, and the cabs just whiz by without paying any attention. Anything could happen."

"And did anything happen?"

No! Manny wanted to scream.

"How would you like a new suit?"

Why didn't the light change? Could he go on red anyway?

"Today you are a man!"

A woman passing said, "Oh, my God, I forgot the pickles! Now I have to go all the way back."

"It was my brother's suit."

"You should have a suit of your own."

"You don't need the pickles," a voice said.

"It wouldn't be a picnic without pickles."

The car took off abruptly from the curb; the man gunned the motor and it roared. Manny felt the hot air of the exhaust drift past him.

*"Homosexuals can't help the way they are. They're born
that way, mister."*

The light changed to green. Manny started to step down
from the curb. The glass vial slipped from his hot, per-
spiring fingers and shattered on the pavement. Manny
looked down and saw the grasshopper scurry away, down
into the underside of the gutter; the roach stayed transfixed, his antennae quivering frantically. With the tip of
the toe of his loafer, Manny gave the roach a little push
to make him go. He could go now; Manny didn't have
anything to carry him in any more. The roach hesitated
still; darted one way, then another, then ran in circles.
The Madison Avenue bus came rumbling to the corner,
puffing and snorting as it stopped within inches of Manny
as he crossed the street. He saw the great round rubber
tires of the bus bear down on the confused cockroach.

"Have a good day, son. Youth is to enjoy."

Ruth Pollack reread the note under "Showing Today"
in the *New York Daily Record*:

LAS VEGAS STORY—(90m. RKO, '52)
Torch-bearing cop, night-club songbird married to
big-shot gambler, sentimental pianist, and sudden
murder. Victor Mature, Jane Russell, Vincent Price,
Hoagy Carmichael. 12:30, 3:50, 7:10, 10:30.

She slapped the newspaper down and scratched an oven
match under the table, touching its flame to her cigarette.
Beside her, on the arm of the stuffed chair facing the television set, was a light-green glass plate holding the crusts
from the cream-cheese-and-jelly sandwich she had just finished. The set was turned on and an old movie was in
wavy view. She looked at her watch and sighed, sucking
on the cigarette, the expression on her thin, tired face one
of acute rage. The cup of coffee next to the glass plate
was half filled, and she raised it to her lips. When the
front door of the apartment slammed, she banged it down
in the saucer.

"Emanuel?"

There was no answer.

Her voice rose. "E-*man*-uel!"

She got up and walked to the hallway, where he stood.
His blank, slow-eyed expression at once aggravated her

anger. She said, "Do you know what time it is, young man? *Do you?*"

"I don't know," he answered. He just stood there like a glob, his dull, lusterless eyes like the eyes of a fish dying on a hook.

"It's a quarter past two!"

"Oh."

"You were finished at a quarter to twelve. Well, we *missed* the movie," she said. "The picture went on at twelve-thirty."

"I'm sorry," Manny said.

"Sorry! You *knew* I wanted to see that picture."

"I'm sorry," Manny mumbled. "You should have gone."

"Alone, I suppose! My own son isn't thoughtful enough to get himself home here in time to go with me. Dawdling! You were dawdling, weren't you?"

Manny shook his head. He turned from her slightly.

"Well, we missed the movie!"

"I'm sorry," he repeated senselessly.

He started to walk back to his room. His mother said something as he was midway down the hall, and he stopped to hear.

She said, "If we went now, we'd get in right in the middle of *Tarzan and the Leopard Woman,* and I'm not going to sit through that trash!" She said, "Well, *my* day is ruined. Thanks to *you,* Emanuel!"

10

Love-bitten, smitten, smitten—
Sittin' in a daze,
Goin' through a phase . . .
—*"Love-Bitten"*

JOHNNY CAME UP THE WALK with his father on that muggy Thursday night, the first week of August. He saw her standing just inside the lobby, waiting for the elevator, and he tried to avoid meeting her eyes.

His father was saying, "What would you say to a vacation, Johnny? You've worked pretty hard this summer. Maybe you'd like the rest of the month off, before school starts again. Would you like that?"

He had his arm clamped affectionately around Johnny's shoulders. They had come home together from the office, where Johnny was helping out as a messenger. He got $1.25 an hour for it, and he was saving to buy parts for a hi-fi he planned to build himself.

"I still have thirty dollars to go," he answered. He had not seen her since that night on the roof.

"Maybe we can work something out so you can have the thirty dollars *and* a vacation," his father said.

Johnny said, "It would be swell if we could, all right."

"I think we can if we put our heads together, John."

She looked up at them when they came into the lobby, and then away. She shifted a carton of root beer from one hand to the other, and pressed the button of the elevator again, although the red light indicated it was on the way down. Her white cotton dress had a tiny violet design; it was sleeveless and flimsy with a full skirt and a lace petticoat that showed a fraction of an inch beneath the hem. She wore the same sandals on her feet, and an infinitesimal gold chain on her bare ankle.

Johnny's father said, "Hello, Lynn."

"Hi, Mr. Wylie . . . J-Johnny."

Johnny said, "Greetings." His tone did not sound as offhand as he had anticipated. He looked down at the carton of root beer. "Getting drunk again t'night, I see," he said.

80

Lynn Leonard giggled, and then looked at his face for the first time. She wasn't mad at him; he could tell.

She said to his father, "How do you like Johnny's 'tash, Mr. Wylie?"

"That's a new name for it," Richard Wylie answered with a smile.

"I *told* her that," Johnny said. "I told her it was a goofy name for a mustache."

"If you want my frank opinion, Lynn, I don't think it adds much." He chuckled. "Maybe you can influence him to take a razor to it. His father certainly can't."

"Me?" the girl said. "Me!" She hit her head with the palm of her hand in a gesture of mock shock. "*I* don't have anything to say far as *Johnny's* concerned."

"Darn right!" Johnny agreed, embarrassed. "Christmas! Christmas and Easter anyhow!"

The elevator reached the lobby then and the three got inside. Mr. Wylie studied his folded newspaper, and Johnny stood off to the far end of the square box, away from her. She looked straight ahead at the door, and he feigned an absorbed interest in his hands, examining them assiduously. After a few moments' silence, she said, "Got any new records lately, Johnny?"

"I got the new Brubeck album," Johnny muttered, intent on his knuckles.

"Is it good?"

"You wouldn't even know who Brubeck is, probably."

"I'd like to hear the music. I like music."

"Me too."

"Johnny?"

"Huh?"

"Could I listen to it sometime? We've got a vic."

"Suits me," Johnny said.

"I've got the Hilltoppers singing 'P.S. I Love You.' I like that one. I've got 'Love-Bitten,' too, by the Three Bells."

"That stuff's too goopy," Johnny said. "I hate a lot of goop."

"I don't mind if it isn't *too* goopy."

" 'Love-Bitten' gives me a big pain you know where," Johnny said. " 'S all you hear all over the place. 'Love-bitten, smitten, smitten.' Musta been Einstein wrote that one, 's got such good lyrics."

Johnny's father folded his newspaper and said, "We set

a record high today. Ninety-seven degrees! That's hot weather, *real* hot weather."

The elevator jerked to a stop and they all got out. Before Lynn turned to walk down to her apartment, she said, "If you're not doing anything tonight, Johnny, it'd be swell to hear your records. Mom and Dad are going to see 'Teahouse of the August Moon.' I got some root beer."

Johnny said, "I don't know whether I'm doing anything or not. If nothing turns up I might lug 'em over. You got three speed?"

"What do you think?" She giggled. "It's the Dark Ages?"

"Who can tell any more?" Johnny said.

After dinner Johnny went back to his room. He snapped on the radio and walked over to his bureau. The room had light-green walls and dark-green curtains and bedspread. There were pictures of Stan Getz, Fats Navarro, Erroll Garner, the Johnny Guarnieri Trio, and Louis Armstrong, which he had sent away for, and which his mother had had framed for his walls last Christmas. They hung in a long straight row over his bed. Attached to the mirror over his dresser there was a piece of dried palm shaped like a cross, which he had saved since last Easter, and a rosary looped over a wooden knob. The words to "Baby, Won't You Please Come Home:?" and "Fine and Dandy" were ripped from a songbook and Scotch-taped to the upper left-hand corner of the mirror. A picture of himself and Flip and Manny, standing with their arms around one another in front of school, was contained in a plastic frame, set next to an old hard orange Johnny had been saving for seven years. Across the top of the photograph of the threesome, Johnny had printed in red ink: "The Three Musketeers, or A Day at the Zoo (Monkey Cage!).

From the radio, a woman's passion-thick voice whispered, "Are you going to leave me like this, Frederick?"

Johnny hooted and slapped his knee. "Yeah, baby," he said, strolling over to turn the dial of the radio, "I'm cutting out on you."

Music filled the room then; a crooner sang, "They try to tell us we're too young, too young to really be in love. . . ." Johnny walked back to the bureau and looked into the mirror. He held his arms out and opened his mouth as though he were singing the song. He screwed his face up in an earnest expression, as though he were the vocalist. He did it until the song ended, and then he smiled winningly. His head bent as if he were receiving applause, and he said to his reflection, "Thank you. Thank you." Then he took his military brushes and ran them through his hair, touching them gently to his mustache. He ambled over to his bed and flopped down on his back.

A knock came at his door, and he called out, " 'Min."

Richard Wylie stood in the doorway, tamping tobacco down into the bowl of a pipe he held in his hand. "Before you go, Johnny," he said, "I thought we might discuss a way you could earn that extra money without working at the office."

"Who says I'm going anyplace?"

"Aren't you going over to Lynn's?"

"That one," Johnny said, pretending disgust. "Cripes, goes around calling a mustache a 'tash."

"Well," his father said, "in any case, shall we talk about it now?"

"Pull up a toadstool," Johnny said.

His father sat down in the chair before Johnny's desk. He lit his pipe and sat back relaxed, his hands resting at the back of his head. "Here's my proposition," he began. "If you'll promise to work out with me a way you can take both music and prelaw courses in school, I'll see that you get the thirty dollars."

"Music courses!" Johnny said. "I don't want to study piano or learn all about long-hair stuff."

"If you're going into the field, fellow, you have to know your stuff. You said that was the field you were interested in."

"I suppose Rodgers and Hammerstein went to college."

"As a matter of fact, they did."

Johnny said, "I bet most of the disc jockeys didn't."

"Those that didn't, fellow, probably wish they had. In any field, John, you've got to know your stuff. Now, I hope you'll eventually change your mind and go into law. That's why I'd like you to carry a prelaw course. But you don't have to go on if you don't want to."

"Don't worry," Johnny said, "I won't."

"But at least start off on the right foot. And take your music right along with it."

"Aw, I don't know," Johnny said. "Cripes, it's so far off."

"Not as far as you think. You're fifteen, John."

"Sweet fifteen."

"Well, what do you say? Will you try to work something out with me?"

"I suppose."

"That's my boy!" Richard Wylie said. He stood up and looked down at Johnny, who was sprawled on the bed. "We might even take a few trips to some of the colleges and look over the campuses. You know, you'll be sixteen in a few months, and I suppose I'll have to teach you how to drive. We could drive up to some of them together this summer."

"Someday I want a little bright-red MG," Johnny said. "They can go like the devil."

His father laughed. "First things first." He dug into his pants pocket and brought out a money clip. He took a five from the pack and put it on Johnny's desk. "That's severance pay, fellow. You're fired."

Johnny said, *"Hot* damn!"

When his father left, Johnny got up and took the bill and reached for his wallet. There were six or seven celluloid slots for pictures and identification cards in the wallet, and Johnny looked them over after he stuffed the five in the money section. There was a picture of his mother and his father and himself, taken three years ago up on Cape Cod. There was an identification card upon which Johnny had written after the words, "In case of accident please notify": "City Morgue." There was a picture of a sad-eyed basset hound, and one of a Mark-5 Jaguar, both cut from magazines. And there was a group picture of Eddie Condon and his orchestra, which he had clipped from *Downbeat.* Johnny closed the wallet, zipped it up, and whistled along with the music over the radio. He got up and walked around the room. He was frowning and snapping his fingers to the rhythm.

"Oh, when the saints!" he sang softly to himself. "Oh, when the saints! Oh, when the saints come march-ing in . . . "

Again he stopped before the mirror and looked at his reflection. He felt his mustache, then opened his lips and looked at his teeth. He stepped back with his arms on his hips and looked fully at himself. He said very seriously, "Hi. I brought my records." Then he turned, crossed the room, and shut off the radio.

"Hi. I . . ."

"Hello, Johnny," she said. "I didn't think you'd come."

"I can't stay long," he said.

"Did you bring your records?"

"What do you think?"

"I don't know, Johnny."

"That's what I came over for, isn't it?" he grumbled.

He walked past her into the large living room. It was furnished nicely, less modern than the Wylies' apartment, leaning toward the early-American style, but warm and comfortable-looking. Johnny had never been inside before. He plopped himself down in a wide, diamond-patterned stuffed chair and said, "One beer. No head, please."

She laughed, her face flushing with some small excitement, and she said, "I'll go into the kitchen and bring us some. I'll only be a minute."

Johnny looked at his watch with an exaggerated swing of his arm. "I'll time you," he said. . . .

It was much later when she suggested they try dancing. They had been sitting opposite each other in that room, awkwardly becoming used to the fact that they were alone there together. Johnny had set up the records on the automatic player and turned the volume up very loud, so that when either said anything, it was necessary to shout, but they did not talk very much. When they did speak, it was only to make some unnecessary comment, to cover up their shy embarrassment. They said:

"Root beer! The Bowery's favorite beverage!"

"I love a trumpet, Johnny. Really! I'd rather listen to a trumpet than anything in the whole world."

"Boy, the joint is jumping tonight, all right."

"Will another drink make you drunk, Johnny?"

They did not look at each other's eyes at all, and they were both painfully aware of this. When she handed him a second glass of the root beer, she held the glass with her fingers near its rim, and he reached for it far down at its base, so that their fingers couldn't possibly meet. Once when she passed him, her skirt brushed his knee, and he jumped back in his seat. Without knowing why, she apologized, and he answered, " 'S O.K."

Once he had looked at her dress, where it dipped down from her throat to the crease between the breasts that he, John Wylie, had touched on the second day of August in the year 1953. She had felt his eyes there, and they had

both become immediately conscious of their own breathing, and, in that swift moment that soon passed, immensely lonely and confused.

Once while the records were changing, a second of silence seemed to split the room in half with its noise.

It was long after all of this had happened and nothing
really had happened that she said, "Why don't we dance,
Johnny? It would be fun."

"I can't dance fast."

"Muskrat Ramble" was coming out loudly over the
speaker. She was already on her feet, and she had kicked
off her sandals.

"I'll teach you. Want to?"

"I'm not the type."

"Yes, you are. You are too!"

"I can't even dance slow. I can't even *dance*."

"I'll teach you, Johnny," she said. "C'mon." She went
to him where he was sitting in the chair and pulled at his
arm. "C'mon."

Grumbling, he got to his feet. He watched her for a
moment while she did a step, and he said, "Uh-uh. I
could never do that."

"Try!"

"It's sort of like this?" He tried.

"That's it. That's good, Johnny."

"It's terrible!" he growled, but he did not stop. Then
she took his hand, and together they were doing the steps,
fast. She was smiling, and he was trying to suppress a
smile, and both of them were glad. They danced faster
and faster. He kept looking anxiously at his feet, and trying to make them go the same way hers went, and she
kept telling him he was good, and she knew he could do
it.

Her quick, agonized scream of pain finished their frenzy.
Johnny had stepped fully on her bare foot with his heavy
leather shoe. She looked as though she would cry, and
Johnny stood helplessly staring at her, his arms dangling
at his sides, his young eyes concerned and sorry.

"It'll be all right," she managed to say, leaning against
the wall, holding her foot up from the floor slightly as she
stood on the other.

"I didn't mean it, Lynn. Does it—" He moved toward
her and said, "I feel *terrible*. I knew I couldn't dance."

"You were doing swell. It's all right. It's nothing." She

pushed herself away from the wall and put weight on the foot. She tested it, and she could walk, and she smiled up at Johnny. "See? It's all right."

The music blared in the background.

Johnny said, "Are you sure?"

"It's fine," she said. "It's like new."

"I'm so clumsy," Johnny said.

"No, you're not," she answered, and she looked into his eyes then. "Johnny?"

Impulsively he took her arms, pulling her to him, and he kissed her on the mouth. He did it in an impatient, rough way, so that their faces came together awkwardly, and their noses bumped. Both of them laughed, and stood apart.

"Our noses got in the way," she said.

"Yours is so darn big!" he said.

"No, *yours* is!"

"Mrs. Jimmy Durante," he teased.

Then they stopped laughing and looked at each other with faces that were puzzled and afraid. Their arms found each other's body, and their lips met, and they kissed for a long time. While he was kissing her, his hand came once again to her breast, and he knew then why she had made a noise like that.

She said, "It's bright in here." He could feel her mouth make the words against his lips.

He said, "Let's turn off some of the lights or something."

She left his arms and walked to the bridge lamp, pulling the light chain. She went to the table and fixed the lamp there so that only one light burned, a soft one that did not give off much illumination. Neither spoke. He followed her to the couch and sat beside her, and they thrust themselves into each other's arms in a sudden hurried moment, as though they feared they would have to talk. He put his hand into the dip of her dress and felt the satin of her bra, and she said his name. He tried to push his hand inside the bra, but it was too tight, and so he just cupped her breast from outside. She said, "The other light, Johnny. Turn it off."

He squeezed her hard, his lips boring into hers, the feeling of her breast unbelievable to him.

"Gee," he said. "Gee, gee . . ."

She said, "The other light."

He got up, crossed the room, and turned it off.

In the darkness she said, "Don't stumble, Johnny."

"I'm O.K."

He had never said "I love you" to anyone before, and when he said it he didn't believe it, but she believed it. He said it because he was scared. They were lying side by side; he had unbuttoned her dress; and his hands fumbled with the hooks on her brassiere. He couldn't get them undone.

She said, "Let me do it," and her voice sounded a long way off from that room. She squirmed and he heard the hooks unsnap, and then he reached out for her.

He moaned, "Oh, my *God!* Oh—my *God,* Lynn!"

He had never thought of touching a girl anywhere but on the breasts, and when he did, it nearly drove him out of his mind with excitement.

She said, "Oh, Johnny, Johnny, Johnny," and he wanted to cry.

He said, "Lynn Leonard," in a strange, thick, amazed tone.

The same record played over and over and they did not hear it. Cozy Cole was on the drums, and it was "Bugle Call Rag," Louis Armstrong's All Stars. It just kept repeating. Neither Johnny nor the girl knew how much time had elapsed before she said, "No! No, Johnny!"

"Lynn, for God's sake! For God's sake!"

"No, no, no! No, please."

"W-why?"

"Not here. Not here. I couldn't. My folks'll be—"

"Gee, Lynn—oh, my gosh."

"No, Johnny. No, let's get up."

"Yeah," he said. He was shaking; his voice shook too. "Yeah."

Then she sat up and he did too. His hair was mussed and he smoothed it with the palms of his hands, and he heard her fumbling with her clothes, and a bugle was playing.

She said, "I guess we ought to turn a light on."

"Cripes," he said. "No."

"I don't know what time it is."

He sat forward on the couch, cradling his head in his hands. He said, "Wow!"

She stood up and turned on a light. Their eyes blinked and squinted in the brightness, and Johnny sighed.

"We've worn out the record," she said, laughing a little unsurely.

"Who cares? Gee."

She said, "I— feel funny."

"So do I."

"I never—"

She did not have to elaborate. Johnny said, "Me neither."

"I guess we shouldn't have done all that. Huh?"

"We didn't do anything," Johnny said.

"Almost, though." She ran over to where he sat on the couch, and, sinking to her knees, she put her head in his lap. "I was scared, Johnny. Johnny, were you?"

"Naw," Johnny lied.

"Men don't get scared, I guess."

His hand reached out tenderly for a lock of her black hair. He smoothed it back from her forehead. "Men are stronger," he said.

"D-do you really love me, Johnny?"

"Sure," he said. "What do you think?"

Johnny left the apartment shortly after that. Before he left they had arranged the matter between them.

"See you next Saturday, then," he said. "I was supposed to go to this dumb party, but I wouldn't of anyway."

"Where can we go, Johnny?"

"I'll think of something," he said. "I'll meet you on the roof."

"Should we?"

"We're in love, aren't we?"

She said, "Yes, but—"

"Besides," he said, "you promised."

"You won't—think less of me, will you, Johnny? I mean—"

"Oh, for Christmas' sake!" Johnny muttered. "Christmas and Easter anyhow, Lynn. I *love* you." Maybe he really did.

II

> "He will hew to the line of right,
> let the chips fly where they may."
> —*Inscription under the picture of
> Bardo Raleigh in the academy annual,*
> The Sands

BARDO CLOSED his copy of *The Sands* and sat back with his feet propped up on the desk in his room. It was drizzling out that Friday afternoon, and whenever it rained, Bardo became moody. Whenever he became moody, he would glance through his old annual and read the long list of activities under his name:

> BARDO ROBERT RALEIGH
> New York, N. Y.
> President, Sword & Shield; Colonel
> of Cadets; President, Drill Team;
> Secretary-Treasurer, Blue & Gold
> Honor Society; Member, E.L.A.,
> The Gold Key, The Blue Masque,
> Scroll Staff; Honor Freshman Cadet
> '50; Honor Sophomore Cadet '51;
> Honor Senior Cadet '53; Clean-up
> Committee.

He would study his picture. It was a good likeness, the only photograph in the book shot in profile. He would sit and think and remember back, plucking incidents from the past and realizing the sudden shock of nostalgia for sundry things like the bugle blowing out taps at ten P.M., inspection of arms in the quadrangle, and the curt bark of a platoon sergeant commanding, "P'toon . . . ten-chht!"

He would stare at walls and window sills and see the soot of the immense city of New York there, and he would recall the way he had run his white-gloved fingers along other walls and sills and said, "I'm pulling you for dirt, mister! This is a pigsty!" And he would feel immediately sorry for himself, and a little sad.

Sometimes he would remember what General Baird had

90

said to him: "You have more responsibility than the average man, Raleigh. You're a leader!"

Other times he would just recall random masculine voices shouting random words that spelled out a way of life:

"Put a 'sir' on that, mister!"

"A-dease!"

"Attention. General leave will begin in ten minutes. Repeat. General leave will—"

"Pull that chin in! Drop those shoulders! Get a wrinkle in that neck!"

This was the myriad music of his musings.

Ivy Raleigh was working in her room that afternoon. He could hear the clatter of her typewriter. She had brought work home from the office, and he had not seen her since lunch.

At lunch she had asked him suddenly, "Bar, dear?"

"Hmmm?"

"Have you by any chance seen my ring?"

"What ring?"

"You know, honey—my old wedding ring. I can't find it."

"That's a pity, Ivy."

"Then you haven't seen it?"

"No."

"You were poking around in my bureau drawers the other night, remember? Last week? Was it there then?"

"Good Lord, Ivy! Why would I want that ring?"

"No, I just wondered if it was there then."

"I haven't the vaguest memory."

"Peculiar."

"Maybe Claude took it."

"Don't be silly, Bar."

"He may have."

"Why would *he* want it?" She'd laughed. "Bar, you *are* silly!"

"For the size. Perhaps he wants to present you with a diamond, dear."

"Oh, Bar! He knows my ring size."

"Does he?"

"Of course, darling."

"Oh," Bardo had answered flatly. "I didn't realize. 'Scuse?"

Bardo had an idea he had been nursing all afternoon.

It was an idea to organize the three boys he had been with last week end; to incorporate the foursome into a sort of police corps. Their business would be to police the parks of the city to rid them of vagrants and vandals. He had even invented a little song they might adopt as their hymn of allegiance and purpose. He had printed it out carefully on a piece of white paper. It could be sung to the tune of the "Battle Hymn of the Republic":

Mine eyes have seen the vagrants on the benches
    in the park.
And the bums that haunt the pathways while
    they're roaming in the dark.
We'll attack them, and we'll beat them, and
    upon them leave our mark,
Then we'll go marching on.

> *Glory, glory, hallelujah!*
> *Glory, glory, hallelujah!*
> *Glory, glory, hallelujah!*
> *Then we'll go marching on.*

There could be three or four more verses to it, about the lovers and the vandals and the juvenile delinquents. He had written only the one. Whenever people were organized it was good to have a song. It gave spirit to the organization. Flip and Manny and Wylie could use some training along these lines. They were too haphazard in their leisure pursuits. Infinitely haphazard.

Another thing that occurred to Raleigh was the fact that the foursome should have a name and a motto. These too he had taken time to invent and print out carefully on a separate piece of white paper:

Name: THE DEFENDERS
Motto: THE BEST DEFENSE IS TO ATTACK.

Bardo tossed his gold pencil on the desk blotter and got up slowly, stretching. He felt groggy; his eyelids were heavy, and he did not try to resist the impulse to sleep any longer. All summer he had been sleeping twelve to fourteen hours a day, intermittently, napping after lunch and dinner and often in the morning after Ivy had left for the office. Carefully he unlaced his shoes, slipped the trees into them, and snapped them secure. His tie he placed on the rack and his shirt on a hanger, along with his pants. In his undershorts he went to the window and pulled the blind, darkening the room; and he opened the window wider for more air. Then he pulled the cover back on the bed and crawled between the sheets. Curling up there, he closed his eyes, and to the persistent tapping of the rain and of the typewriter in Ivy's room Bardo dreamed:

The play was about a king and queen, and from his seat in the theater, Bardo could see the queen's face very clearly. He said to Manny, who was sitting with him, "That's Ivy, you know," and then Manny was not sitting there at all, but his snake was there, and Bardo couldn't get it to come to him. The king had no face, but he was kissing Ivy on the stage. Bardo decided to go backstage when the performance was over. Then when he looked at his clothes he saw they had turned to rags; and his legs and arms were encrusted with filth. Horrified, he began to scream. . . .

"Darling?"

"Hmmm?"

"I thought I heard you calling."

He sat up in bed, rubbing his eyes.

"I'm sorry, Bar. I woke you up."

"It doesn't make any difference," he said.

She sat near his desk, pulling the blind a bit; the rain splashed against the window. "You know, honey, I've been wanting to talk to you about something."

Bardo wrapped the sheets around his legs, covering his shorts.

He said, "Sure."

"Sometimes I think you're intuitive, Bar."

"Why so?"

"Well . . . do you remember what we talked about this noon?"

"I'm not *that* intuitive. You probably just misplaced the ring."

"No, darling. I mean, about what you said with regard to Claude? Do you remember? You said perhaps he wants to give me a ring."

"And?"

"And—" She smiled and shrugged her shoulders. "He *does.*"

"Oh," Bardo said flatly.

"Bar, Claude is being reassigned. He's been offered a very fine new position on the West Coast."

"Bright fellow, Mr. McCoy."

"In San Francisco."

"The Golden Gate."

"He wouldn't go until sometime in late October."

"Really?"

"Bar?"

He didn't look at her. "What?"

"Can't you guess what I'm trying to tell you?"

"Of course!"

There was a pause and Ivy Raleigh looked out of the window at the rain. Then she said, "You like Claude, don't you, Bar?"

"It's Claude that doesn't like me."

"He's immensely fond of you, Bar. I want you to believe that, because it's true."

"Are you going to marry him, then?"

"After you go away, it'll be—well, Bar, you'll start growing away from me and—"

"And you're going to marry him."

"I'm considering it, Bar . . . yes."

"What do you want to do about it?" he said.

"I want you to be *happy* about it."

"Very well," Bardo said. "Bardo Robert Raleigh takes pleasure in announcing the fact that he is infinitely happy at the fact that you are considering marriage with one McCoy, name of Claude."

She looked at him for a moment, puzzled; then she laughed. He was sitting up in bed there with the sheet around him, an eyebrow cocked, a quizzical grin tipping his lips.

"Oh, *darling*," she said, getting up and going over to him. "You're a tease!" She bent and hugged him. "For a moment you had me thinking that I was going to have a problem."

12

He never cared how we felt. He disgraced us before friends and neighbors. And now he has disgraced us again.

—*Statement made to reporters by Peter Heine*

BEHIND HIS HORN-RIMMED GLASSES, Leemie's eyes were sympathetic that Saturday morning, and he said, "You got a right to be a blue boy every now and then, man. You got that right."

"I'm cutting out," Flip Heine told him. "And I'm going to cut out wide. Out of this stinking city! Away from this place!"

He was sitting on the edge of the iron bed in Leemie's room, the cap pulled down on his head. His eyes were bloodshot from crying, and the handkerchief Leemie had lent him was balled up in his hand.

"Where you gonna go, man?"

"I'm never going back."

"You had it!"

"Jesus, Leem, did your old man ever pull anything like this on *you?*"

"He raised me right," Leemie said. "*I* goofed. I didn't go for the readin', writin', 'rithmetic routine. You know? Like, I didn't dig the stuff. I had eyes for the numbers outside books."

Flip wadded the handkerchief into his pocket. "My old man thinks the place is all I got to know about, all I got to think about. I'd just as soon gone to college. You know? Yale. Class!"

"Mine raised me right," Leemie repeated.

"Be a lawyer or something big deal. Friend of mine's going to be a lawyer. My old man thinks Yale's the name of a lock."

"He had you under lock and key, didn't he, man?"

"No more," Flip said, pulling the cap down farther toward his ears. "I checked out for final this time."

Leemie walked over to the old maple bureau and pulled out a drawer. He fumbled for an envelope and a small square package of tissue. "Yeah," he said, "but the break ain't all that easy to make. You got to have moola, man! Everything costs."

"Why couldn't I work for you, Leem? Till I got enough?"

"No dice," Leemie said. He sat down in the rocker near the window and began to roll some of the ground-up weed he took from the envelope into the tissue. "Runaway kid around, I'd get hung, man. A few days you can stay, O.K., but I can't use a permanent roommate."

"Who'd know, Leem?"

"Some wise dick. No dice." Leemie brought the tissue to his mouth, licked an end, and rolled it up tight to make a cigarette.

"You smoking tea?" Flip asked him.

"Yeah. A little pot now and then picks up the pieces."

"I never had any of the stuff. Once in school they give us this big lecture, see, all about how it makes you squirrely."

"Makes squirrels out squirrels," Leemie said. He struck a match and lit up, sucking the smoke into his nostrils and sniffing it up into his head.

"What's it make you feel like, anyhow?"

"No way. That's the kick."

"You just sail, huh, Leem?"

"Man, you don't go no place. You stay."

"Can I have a drag?"

"No dice. It costs. Can't hardly make a strike these days with all the Fridays out smellin' the air."

"What's it cost?" Flip asked.

"A packet like this? Four fin."

"Man!"

"A buck a stick, rolled."

Leemie sat there sniffing the smoke up his nose, while Flip Heine began walking back and forth across the room with his hands jammed into the pockets of his best trousers. On the floor under the bed there was a duffel bag he had filled that morning. In it were four shirts; another pair of pants; two pairs of undershorts, one dirty, one clean; socks, a toothbrush, a half-dozen comic books, and his Social Security card. He had stolen out of his family's apartment early that morning, between four and five, after he had finished work at the place and everyone was in bed asleep. Until dawn he rode the Lexington Avenue subway, up to the end and back down and up again. Then he'd bought a cup of coffee and a bagel and headed for Leemie's. It was the only place he could think to go where he wouldn't be ashamed.

Flip was afraid, but he didn't tell Leemie that. He told him everything that had happened all week; why his father had done it to him; and what his mother had whispered to him afterward in her slow German, her hand on his brow as he lay forlorn on his bed.

> *"Schön ist's vielleicht anderswo,*
> *Doch hier sind wir sowieso."*

Flip had thought about that a lot:

> "It might be nice some other place,
> But here we are in any case."

It hadn't offered him much consolation at the time, and as he recalled it now, it made him more afraid; and it was this he could not discuss with Leemie. It was knowing he had run away to nothing; no one; just run away, and here he was. Where? And what would he do now?

He had not really wanted to stay and work for Leemie. Leemie was too different, too weird. But when Leemie had said "No dice" to his suggestion, it had been like the closing of a final door. Manny and Johnny and Bardo couldn't help him; he wasn't even going to tell them about it. How could he? Their folks weren't like that. Manny hadn't even caught hell for flunking his subjects. Flip would have been black and blue for that alone. Johnny's father wanted him to go to college, and Bardo called his mother by her first name. Even a creep like Leemie saw the fact that Flip must have some lousy family to do a thing like that to a guy.

"You mean just 'cause you didn't get a haircut?" Leemie'd said, amazed.

And Flip had broken down and bawled like a fruit.

Leemie'd said, "It'll grow back, man." He'd slapped Flip across the shoulder. "You ain't permanently bald or nothin' like that, man. 'Sides, can't hardly tell the difference with the cap on."

"Shaving a man's goddamn head this way," Flip had cried. "Jesus!"

The harsh and pungent smell of the marijuana that Leemie was smoking made Flip feel kind of sick. He saw the pictures stuck in Leemie's mirror, and the books he had stacked in dusty corners around the small room, and the dirty sink with the rusty fixtures, and the soap scum stuck around the bowl. He wondered vaguely what his mother and father and his brothers and sisters would be saying now about him being gone; and he thought of the way his mother scrubbed every floor in the flat every day, on her hands and knees.

"Man," Leemie said, "don't look like that phone's going to ring."

"It'll ring," Flip said, "or I'll try the number again later."

"You act kind of rifty. You all right?"

"What do you think?" Flip said.

It would be dark, and maybe they wouldn't be able to tell with his cap on. He'd chance it anyway. He couldn't just stay cooped up at Leemie's day and night. Besides, that was the only thing he knew he wanted to do now: cruise around with the three of them the way they'd done last week. Someday, he bet, Bardo Raleigh would be a big man and his name would be in all the papers. A general even, maybe. Him a general, Johnny a lawyer, and Manny the head of the S.P.C.A. or something. Christ!

He said, "Even if I went back, it wouldn't be any good. I'd catch more hell."

Leemie blew smoke through his nose. "You still owe me for the knife," he said, "but I ain't gonna kick your teeth in when you're down."

"All of a sudden everything's so goddamn crazy," Flip mused. He socked the air with his fist.

"It'll grow back," Leemie said.

Peter Heine rapped the dottle from his pipe hard against the old black stove. Behind him in the kitchen his wife spread the plates out on the table.

"No," he said, "we don't tell anyone."

"He packed a *Patentkoffer,* Peter."

"He'll come back. Why should we announce we have such a son? Announce to the world we cannot control him. How do we look then?"

"It was his hair, Peter. I think he was ashamed."

"So he would go to show the world? No! Defiance he goes to show the world!"

"He had no money," the old woman said. "Where can he go?"

"To his store, maybe. To his dirty store!"

Peter Heine kicked a chair out from the table and sank down on it. He tucked a white napkin into his shirt collar and reached for a piece of dark bread.

"We could send Karl to look," his wife said.

"Karl has his work! Is the place to close down because we have an ingrate for a son?"

"I could go."

"Where is the store? Who knows that? *Ja!* His store is a secret even from his family!"

"I could look in the stores along the street," the old woman said. She padded to the stove on slippered feet, reached for a ladle, and stirred soup in the huge tin pot. "I could look in all of them," she said, "and maybe find him."

"And find the devil's tongue to gossip, maybe too you would!"

"*Ja!* The devil has a long tongue."

"He'll come home, he will, and I'll break his *legs* this time, and we'll see how far he runs!"

"No more fighting, Peter. You must promise."

"I must promise I want my son a fool? I must promise I want him out in the streets getting into trouble? No! He *has* to *learn!*"

"Young hearts listen little and learn slow," Hans Heine's mother mused.

His father said, "The whip will teach what words will not!"

But here we are in any case, Flip thought. It was hot and the stale air was close. Leemie slept in a pair of ragged jockey shorts on the bed, his skinny body rising and falling with his heavy breathing, a book called *The Duchess Instructs Her Ladies in the Art of Love* fallen to the floor, worn pages spilling from between its crude yellow paper covers.

Flip peeled an orange and sucked the juice out of it, looked at the clock and saw it was past noon, and wondered why he cared what time it was. His mother used to have an expression, "Watched pots never boil." Maybe she had already called the police and they were out looking for him. Maybe they'd nab him when he left Leemie's and make him go back home. Aw, it wouldn't do any good even if they did. His old man would probably kill him this time.

Walking over to the window, Flip rubbed the smudge from a narrow pane and looked out on the hot street. A fire hydrant was uncapped, and kids were dancing in and out of the flow of water, squealing and laughing and having a good time. The water gushed down the sewers, carrying bits of paper and odd pieces of garbage with it. A moth-eaten mongrel stood barking excitedly on the curb. Three girls were gaily skipping rope. Flip heard them chanting in their singsong, steady tone:

"First comes love and second marriage.
Then comes me and the baby carriage."

Flip turned his back on the window. He stood in the room looking at Leemie, and the dirty book that had dropped to the floor, and sticking out from under the bed the duffel bag with his things in it. Then in the immense complexity of home-longing he thought of his father without rancor, and his eyes filled with stinging tears, and he wanted to know how he could go home again. How could he do it? Just walk in?

The phone cut across his consciousness. Leemie groaned and rolled over.

"Bardo Robert Raleigh here," the voice said. "Did you call me?"

"It's me. Flip."

"Ah, Heine! I tried to reach you earlier."

"I'm not home," Flip said. "D'you call my home?"

"Yes, mister, I did. I wanted to check on tonight."

"What'd they say?"

"That you were out, of course."

"That all they said?"

"That was the extent of our conversation, mister. They said you were out and I could call back again."

"Oh. Yeah, like, they didn't sound worried, huh?"

"Infinitely calm, mister. Now about tonight? You'll be joining us, of course?"

"Crazy!" Flip said dully.

"Then listen!" Bardo commanded.

In the background Leemie snarled at him to get the hell off the phone while Bardo's voice sang:

"Glory, glory, hallelujah!
Glory, glory, hallelujah!
Glory, glory, hallelujah!
Then we'll go marching on."

"Shake it, Hairy Hans," Leemie insisted again angrily. "This ain't tea time."

At the word "tea," Flip's eyes fell to the chair and the half-full packet of marijuana on it. He remembered what Leemie had said. A packet like that cost four fin.

"How'd you like the song, mister?"

"It was crazy, man." Where did a guy sell the stuff, though?

"C'mon, Hairy-head, shake that phone!"

"I've got to cut out now, Bardo."

"See you at nine-thirty, mister. Ninety-sixth and Fifth. Near the entrance to the children's park."

Flip repeated, "Near the entrance to the children's park," and hung up.

"Did your hair grow back while you was talkin' on that telephone, man?" Leemie laughed.

"Yeah," Flip said, thinking maybe a guy could sell stuff like that in a pool hall. "In fact, I gotta get it cut. You know?"

13

In a report issued by Dr. Martha Mannerheim, psychologist with the Jewish Children's Clinic, to whom the patient was sent and with whom he consulted for a brief period (three one-hour sessions), some insight is offered into the traumatic experience the patient underwent on the day the act of violence was subsequently committed. I relate it here in direct quotes. . . .

—*From the psychiatric history of Emanuel Pollack*

THAT SATURDAY AFTERNOON when he left the zoo and headed downtown on the subway to Dr. Mannerheim's, Manny thought about it again. The box on his lap, with air holes punched in the side of it, contained Sincere, and Manny held it there as firmly and carefully and gently as though there were a freshly baked layer cake inside. Actually he had thought about it all week, until even his father had noticed something was different about him, and had said, "Is visiting that psychologist making you mope around this way, Emanuel? I'm not sure it's a good thing for you at all. Young people got enough trouble in this world."

His mother had said that was why he was going to the psychologist in the first place, to see what the trouble *was*.

Manny didn't tell them about the man in the park, but he kept thinking about it. Why had the man picked him, Manny Pollack? What had there been about him that had made the man choose him? Was there something that marked him as different from other people?

He had two peculiar notions that seemed to him to be more pernicious than peculiar. One was that the man had known that Manny had come from the doctor's; had perhaps waited for Manny outside the apartment house on Central Park West, and followed him into the park. The man had thought, maybe, that Manny was visiting a psychologist because *that* was what was wrong with him.

The other was an even more fearful notion: that perhaps Dr. Mannerheim herself had planted the man there, to test Manny—to see if Manny was that way. (And he had flunked the test—gone with the man, let the man give him a ride home afterward! God!)

In a way, it was as though life were one big trap and Manny was walking smack into it; and in another way it was as though life were just a whirlpool and Manny was perpetually spinning around in it without ever coming to any stopping point. If it were not for Sincere, Manny believed, there would be nothing of his own that he could know and have and understand.

Manny raised the top of the box a crack and looked in at his pet. "We're almost there, boy," he whispered, patting the sides of the box tenderly. "Then we won't move for a while and you can sleep."

Having Sincere along with him that afternoon made Manny feel somehow more safe. Not many people knew very much about snakes, and Manny knew all about them. How many people had snakes of their own?

If Sincere were to be set loose in the park, everyone would probably scream, and someone would probably want to throw a rock at him. It was because no one really gave snakes a chance, or thought they had feelings, or knew they only meant to try to live as best they could in this world, because they weren't as smart or friendly as dogs, for instance.

Nothing's going to happen to you, Sinny, Manny thought to himself. I'm going to take care of you the rest of my life. He held the box more tightly, and looked down at it with affection.

It was strange, Manny mused, that Dr. Mannerheim liked snakes too. Women especially never did. But she did; and the first time he had ever gone to her, she had listened to him tell her all about Sincere. She had been interested. She had not interrupted him or smirked or doubted him or patronized him; and Manny remembered that at the end of that hour everything his mother had ever inferred about his "morbid interest" in snakes seemed unimportant. Dr. Mannerheim and Bardo Raleigh were the only two people Manny had ever met (outside zoo-keepers) who seemed to like to hear ·him discuss Sinny, and snakes in general. Johnny and Flip never had much to say when the subject came up. But at both sessions Dr. Mannerheim had *asked* Manny about Sincere, and Bardo had told him a million thousand times he ought to be a herpetologist.

Walking down Central Park West, after he got off the Eighth Avenue subway, Manny decided that his notion about the doctor planting the man in the park was crazy. A person who liked snakes that well wouldn't pull a dirty trick like that on a guy. He was sorry he had ever thought of it; particularly if she ever read it in his mind or some other darn thing. He would be careful not to think about any of it while he was there.

Maybe things like that just happened to people without any reason at all; to *anybody*. Maybe . . . Manny bet Bardo would know. He might ask him when he saw him that night; even just coming out and ask him. You could do that with Bardo, and he'd *tell* you. Bardo always told you.

The sun was out and Manny started to whistle a march he had heard somewhere, and he didn't feel too bad at all. He walked into the apartment house lobby, poked the elevator button with his finger, and looked at a little girl pushing a toy auto across the lobby. While he waited, he leaned down and said, "Hi!"

"Brrrrrrrrr," the girl said, imitating a motor running.

"That's a pretty car," Manny told her.

"Not a car. 'S a bus."

Manny laughed. "I guess I was too dumb to see that," he said.

The little girl looked up at him, a finger caught in her mouth.

"What you got in the box?"

"Oh," Manny said, "a new suit."

A silly little kid like that would be scared of a snake.

"I got a new dress," the girl said.

Manny ruffled her hair playfully, and got into the elevator. Maybe he'd tell Dr. Mannerheim about the little girl. It would be a good topic of conversation when they ran out of things to say. The doctor never seemed to be able to think up any new subjects. Besides, not everybody liked kids or treated them nice. Lots of guys Manny knew would have said that it was *so* a car, that it wasn't a bus

at all. Lots of guys Manny could think of would have
tried to dangle the snake over her head and make her
bawl or something. They wouldn't have been considerate
like Manny. He'd handled the whole thing pretty neatly.
. . . Hadn't he?

She was wearing some kind of light cherry-colored
dress, and she was smiling. Not until Manny saw her in
the doorway when she answered the bell did he realize he
was looking forward to their talk. Again he blamed himself for ever in the world thinking she had sicked that
man on him; a thing like that could happen to anyone.
Deliberately he put it out of his mind, because she had
a way of looking him right square in the eye, as though
she could fathom what he was thinking. All Manny
wanted to do was show her Sincere, and he realized a
little guiltily that his mother didn't know he had taken
the snake with him, because she was in Yonkers for the
day, and she wouldn't be home until after dinner.

Before she had left she had directed Manny: ". . . and
don't sit like a dummy when you get there. How's the
doctor going to help you if you don't tell her what you
brood about all the time?"

Manny followed the doctor through the hallway into
the living room. There were two Cokes on the coffee
table, two glasses, and a bowl of ice cubes. Manny sat
down on the couch and put his box on the floor between
his legs. She leaned back in her chair and lit a cigarette.

She said, "What would you say to a Coke?"

"I guess so," Manny said. He didn't reach for the bottle in front of him.

"Oh? You don't sound very enthusiastic."

"Sure, I want one," Manny said. "One won't hurt."

"*One* won't hurt?"

"You know," Manny answered, grabbing the neck of
the bottle and pouring the coca-cola over an ice cube he
had plunked into the glass, "they're supposed to do something to your teeth."

"Really?"

"Sure. They rot them."

The doctor gave a little laugh and Manny looked over
at her questioningly. "Didn't you ever hear that?"

"N-no," she said. "But—"

"They rot your teeth. Cokes rot your teeth."

She told him he didn't have to drink it, and he said

that was all right. He said, "I didn't say it to make you feel bad."

"I'm sure you didn't."

Manny said, "I just came from the Bronx Zoo. I took Sincere up so the man there could see him. I took him up once before but the man wasn't there. Only *today* he was."

"Oh?" She nodded pleasantly. "And what did he say?"

"He told me how to make the cage warm for him this winter. My room gets kind of chilly, and the temperature's very important. You see, kings catch cold easy."

Manny reached down beside him where the box was and he said, "Did you notice I was carrying something when I came in?"

"Yes."

"Well," Manny said, suddenly a little bashful now, but proud too, and anxious to see the doctor's surprise, "it's Sincere. I got him with me. Want to see him?"

The doctor's face was placid and she said, hesitating only for a moment, "Certainly I want to see him. I've heard so much about Sincere."

Manny took the top off the box and lifted Sincere up, and Sincere wrapped his long body around Manny's arm and flicked his forked black tongue. Dr. Mannerheim sat quietly in her chair, drawing the smoke in from her cigarette, looking at the snake.

"I'll put him down here on the table so you can see him in the light," Manny said, pushing aside the glasses, placing the writhing snake there. "Lookit him now. Isn't he a beauty?"

The snake trailed his black slackness soft-bellied down over the edge of the table, and Manny shoved him back up on top of it.

"Stay there, fellow," Manny said. "The doctor wants to look you over, boy. See if you got any complexes." Manny chuckled and glanced at the doctor, who was moving her chair slightly back from the table. "Like him?" Manny asked, pleased.

"He's f-fine," the doctor said, but she edged her chair farther back, and her face was a little taut, her fingers tightening on the sides of her chair. "Sh-should he be loose like this, Emanuel? It won't make him nervous or upset or anything?"

"Naw!" Manny exclaimed. "Sincere's a real trooper!

He's been on the subway and everything today. He's a world traveler, aren't you, fellow, hmmm?" Manny gave Sincere a pat, and beamed at him with bright, shining eyes.

The snake lopped around the bowl containing the ice cubes, flicked his forked tongue again, and arched his hose-shaped head up in a curve, his dead eyes musing a moment, his body still.

" 'At's right, boy, you look the joint over." Manny laughed. "Lookit him! He wonders where he is. What a curious character you are, Sinny, boy. Lookit him, Dr. Mannerheim."

"I'm looking at him," the doctor said in a strained voice, but Manny didn't notice that her tone was different this time from any other.

He said, "Want to pet him? He's got real silky skin."

"N-no, Emanuel—thanks. I haven't washed my hands and—"

"Oh, your hands are clean enough, Doc. Cripes, your hands are plenty clean. Don't you worry 'bout that."

"No, Emanuel, really," the doctor said, as Manny started to steer Sincere's body around to the edge of the table facing her. "I think not!"

Then Manny noticed. He looked at her strangely, as if there were something about her sound that he could not understand, and he said incredulously, "Is something wrong about Sincere?"

"Emanuel, don't be silly. Of course not. I—I like Sincere. You know I like him." She kept staring at the wiggling snake. "We've talked about him so often, Emanuel. You know I—"

"But you never saw him before," Manny said in a thick sort of voice. "Today was the first time and you're acting funny. You're acting funny," Manny said, as though he weren't really talking to her, but to himself now, still looking at her. "You're acting like other people."

The doctor's face was pale, and her lips moved to protest with the right words, but the snake slid off the table then, writhing like lightning, a part of him that was left behind convulsing in undignified haste and then disappearing to the floor.

"Emanuel!" the woman called out, jumping quickly from the chair and backing away. "Get him! Don't let him loose like this, Emanuel. Emanuel!"

For a moment Manny was frozen numb. He saw Sincere gliding on the thick carpet, innocuously going along the way he did all the time, the way he was made to do, moving on his ribs the way a snake does, because there's no other way for him to move, and then he saw the woman's face. There was nothing soft about her any more; her brow was creased in hard lines and her lips tightened. Her voice had a shrill edge on it:

"Get him back in the box, Emanuel!" she said. "Will you get that snake!"

Manny just stood there. "You hate him," he said. "You hate him because he's a snake. You didn't mean it when you said you liked snakes. You wanted to trick me." He said it the way a person who has to convince himself of something says things, the way a person says things when he can't believe them, because he does not want to. "You're *afraid* of him. You never even listened when I explained he couldn't hurt you," Manny mumbled. "You never even—"

Sincere was near her now, and she screwed up her face and shook the chair and tried to scare him off with the motion. Then Manny moved. There was a vacant look to his eyes, as though he were sleepwalking, and his body moved that way too, stiffly, but surely, crossing the room, past her where she stood near the wall, cowering.

"He's under the couch, Emanuel," she said.

Manny said flatly, "I know where he is, Dr. Mannerheim."

Then he got down on his knees and picked Sincere up gently, saying, "C'mon, fellow," and he carried him to the box, and he put him in it.

He stood there holding the box, and though he did not look at the doctor, he could tell she was smoothing her hair with her hands, moving away from the wall where she was standing; and he heard her sigh. It seemed a long while before she said, "Our session wasn't very successful today, was it, Emanuel?" She sounded sad somehow, and tired.

"I don't know about sessions. I don't know about them," Manny answered her. He ran his fingers along the box, caressing it, as though that would soothe the snake inside. He wouldn't look at the doctor; he couldn't and he didn't want to.

"You see, Emanuel, we try to hide our fears sometimes

to help other people. But we still have them. They're only masked and—"

Manny didn't listen to her. He didn't care what she told him now; he didn't even hear her voice. Sincere was moving in the box and that was the only thing Manny cared about; that was what life all boiled down to—Sincere.

"Do you understand, Emanuel?" she asked him ten years later.

Manny shook his head silently.

"And we're still friends?"

Manny shrugged.

"You think about what I said, Emanuel, and next Tuesday we'll try to talk it over together." She said, "I won't keep you any longer today."

Manny nodded.

At the door, she offered her hand when she said goodby, but Manny was holding the box with both of his.

. . . and so, ladies and gentlemen, one week after their first venture into the park, these four had a second, final rendezvous. What was it that each boy looked forward to as he made his way there so determinedly? It is a tragic and deplorable fact that Bardo Raleigh, Hans Heine, John Wylie, and Emanuel Pollack, four most unlikely companions, were seeking one and the same thing—a kick, ladies and gentlemen, a thrill. And the only way they could find this thrill was through violence.

—*Prosecuting Attorney Leogrande's summary*

IN THE POOL HALL some wise guy had swiped his cap and called him Goldilocks, and he had been afraid to try to sell the stuff. It was still in his back pocket. Now he had no money; only fourteen cents, because he had spent a half a buck on another cap, and sixty-four cents was all he had had when he'd gone to Leemie's. What the hell was he going to do? He could never go back to Leemie's. He didn't even have enough to ride out the night on the subway. In a pawnshop up on 120th Street he'd tried to sell his duffel bag and everything in it, and the man had said, "You kidding, Bud? You couldn't pay me to take this crap!"

He was hungry. He had drunk all the water he could to fill his stomach, and he had his pants belt as tight as it would go.

It was the worst time in his life. And it was hot. It was so hot his whole head was dripping with sweat under his cap. He was tired because he hadn't slept, and he was scared ever to go home again, and scared not to.

He was coming down from 120th, on his way to meet Bardo and Manny and Johnny, and he knew he wouldn't have the nerve to tell them about it, to ask them for a buck or two, or a bed for the night, or food. He would rather tell *anybody* but them.

That night, all Flip Heine wanted to do was hang around with them, keep up the act, and never let them know that his heart was as shorn of hope as his head was of hair.

Emanuel Pollack wanted to take his snake home. He was afraid something would happen to it. It was in the box under the bench in the children's park, where he sat beside Bardo, waiting for Flip. He had gone to Bardo's directly after he left Dr. Mannerheim's office, and Bardo had said:

"That snake, mister, is the most handsome creature Bardo Raleigh ever laid eyes on! Notice the way he winds himself around my arm? Do you know what that is? That's grace, mister. Your Sincere is infinitely graceful."

Manny had telephoned his father to receive permission to eat dinner with Bardo, and he and Bardo had eaten in the Raleighs' kitchen, while Sincere roamed around the linoleum floor.

"Always take care of that snake, Pollack," Bardo had said. "People who neglect their pets and go off and leave them—people like that are the scum of the earth, mister."

"Don't worry, I know that, Bardo."

"You bring him right along with us tonight, mister."

"I ought to take him home first, Bardo."

"You bring him along, mister. That's the best thing."

"You can come with me if I take him home."

"Pollack?"

"What?"

"Why do you suppose I asked you to bring him along? Do you suppose it was because I'd eat my heart out while you were running home with your snake?"

"No, I just thought—"

"Mister, I was wet-nursed and weaned some time ago."

"I know that, Bardo."

"No, you don't, mister. You don't know that at all. You only know what I tell you. And I tell you if you care a tinker's damn for your pet, you'll just bring him along, Pollack, and keep an eye on that priceless creature."

"You really like him, don't you, Bardo?"

"Anyone in his right mind would appreciate the infinite majesty of that snake, Pollack. Anyone in his right mind!"

Manny had said, "You bet they would! Sinny's just like his name, all right. A king!"

Now all Emanuel Pollack wanted to do was to take Sincere home, and then come back and have fun.

Still he sat there, trying to learn the words to the song Bardo was teaching him.

Mine eyes have seen the vagrants on the benches in
        the park
And the bums that haunt the pathways while they're
        roaming in the dark . . .

What made him remember the first time he had ever seen one? What made him think of that evening in Trevor Park up in Yonkers, when he had gone for a walk with his grandmother? How old had he been, and why did he remember it now?

He had a yo-yo, a yellow one, and he couldn't work it, so they sat on a bench and his grandmother tried to show him how. She said, "You just let it go up and down, Bardy. See? Like this." And then she said, "You aren't even watching me, Bardy. Watch me."

But he was watching something else, something across from them—a man stretched out on the bench across from them.

How come he could remember so clearly?

The man was asleep, his arm dangling toward the ground. A battered hat with stains on the band dropped from his fingers. He wore a white shirt that had vomit dried to the front of it and a collar ringed black. The rolled sleeves exposed flesh that was filthy and scaling. And the pants! Baggy brown, ripped at the knees, open in front, where he held his hand. There was a smell from him so foul and strong that it had made Bardy Raleigh want to gag. And the man's nose was running, his mouth agape.

"You aren't even watching me, Bardy."

"What's that man, Gran? Is that man sick?"

"Don't look at him, child."

"Is he sick, Gran?"

"No. No, Bardy. He's just a bum."

A bum?

What was a bum?

Why did it have a familiar sound? And who had said it to Bardy Raleigh before?

He sat there in the darkness on the roof saying her name to himself: "Lynn Leonard."

After tonight he wouldn't be a kid any longer. He wouldn't know a day such as this day had been ever again.

It had started when he had answered the telephone in the morning and told Bardo Raleigh he wouldn't be along with him and Manny and Flip, because he had an appointment. His mother had asked after he'd hung up, "Where's your appointment tonight, Johnny?"

And he had answered, "I'm taking Lynn Leonard to a movie."

"Well, that's very nice."

He'd checked the papers for a movie he could say they'd been to, planning how he'd get the blanket up on the roof, and the pillow, and the pop he was going to buy.

In the afternoon he'd gone across town to a strange neighborhood drugstore and asked for one.

"They come in a package, Romeo," the clerk had kidded him, and the worst thing about it was that the clerk looked about the same age as Johnny.

"I don't know what size," Johnny had mumbled.

"You don't know *nuthin'*, bub! You think they come in sizes?"

Johnny didn't know, but there was the night to come. And then he would, and it would all be different from this day on.

He shut his eyes and wondered how it would be.

First they would talk (what would they say?) and sit side by side without kissing or even holding hands or anything. They would talk and look up at the stars, and he would be able to smell her perfume; and every sentence she would say would have his name at the beginning or the end.

They would lie back with their heads on the pillow, and her black hair would spill onto his white shirt. Their fingers would touch, lightly, then more tightly, and somewhere a radio they wouldn't hear would be playing in the summer air.

Turning, they would face each other, and look into each other's eyes, and he would touch her then, and kiss her and then it would begin. (Should he explain to her that he had one with him? Did men say that?)

He sat there in the darkness on the roof thinking about it and saying her name and his name together; and he thought that when he was eighteen he would ask her to marry him.

He sat there listening for her footsteps, imagining that he heard them, watching the sky, and waiting.

And he waited, and he waited. He waited a long, long time, because he had believed her when she had promised, and he didn't want to believe what he was finally forced to admit—that she wasn't going to come at all.

15

These are not murderers, gangsters. These are children who went looking for mischief and found it.
—*Summary of defense counsel*

THEY STOOD INSIDE the children's park by the swing. After they had sung the song two or three times together, Bardo said suddenly to Heine, "Say, mister, what happened to your hair?" He scrutinized him carefully in the half-light from the street lamp.

Heine grinned broadly. "Man, like, I cut it off!" He felt his head around the sides of the cap. "You know?" he said. "Big gag!"

"What'd you do *that* for, Flip?" Manny asked.

"Big gag, I told you! Wonder what Wylie's doing. Why ain't he coming?"

"He has another engagement," Bardo said. "Now, let's proceed. We'll sing *sotto voce.*"

"I thought we were going to sing *your* song," Flip said.

"*Sotto voce* means 'quietly,' Heine."

"It'd only take me a minute to run home with Sinny, Bardo," Manny said as Bardo started to lead them from the park, up toward the pathway between the road and the reservoir.

Bardo whirled and snapped, "Look, mister, I'm losing patience with you!"

"I only thought—well, I have to keep carrying this box, Bardo."

"When a man carries something he loves, Pollack, it should seem to him to be the lightest thing in the world."

"Hey, that's pretty good, man. You read that somewhere?"

"Gee, Bardo, I never thought of that. I mean—"

"Onward!" Bardo said glibly. "Singing as we go.' '

"Whata we need to sing for?" Flip said as he followed Raleigh.

Bardo answered evenly, "Because, Heine, we're not a

115

pack of disorganized hooligans. We're on serious business tonight. A mission!"

Heine agreed, "Crazy!"

"Look!" Manny said, holding one hand around the box, his free hand pointing up at the summer sky and the stars clustered there in thick, brilliant patches. "The Dippers are out, both of them, and there's Orion. He's the hunter. My brother Irv knew all about that stuff."

"He must have been an astute observer," Bardo commented. "Very few people know anything about Orion."

"That's for sure, man. I didn't even dig the name."

"Sure," Manny said. "You can always tell Orion by those three bright stars there. See them? All in a row. That's his hunting belt."

"Yeah?" Flip said. "Geez, all the things to know in the world. You just never could know all the things."

"Orion," Bardo said in his flat monotone, "is probably the most famous hunter in all of classic mythology. He cleared a whole island of wild, filthy beasts. He used a club for the purpose. He clubbed those loathsome beasts!"

"The island began with the letter D—Dios, or something like that," Manny said.

Flip said, "I heard of Dios."

"It did not, mister. It began with C. It was the island of Chios, where Homer lived."

"Sure," Flip said. "I heard of Homer. Who hasn't? Like, in school and everything. You know?"

"You would have liked my brother, Bardo," Manny said. "He knew things like that, too. Irving would just bring books home and read them. Not for book reports or anything. Just for fun. I mean, he liked it."

Raleigh gave Pollack an affectionate slap across the shoulders. He said, "And you study herpetology, Pollack, because you like it, and Heine here studies the intricate language of jazz."

"Gee." Manny's voice brightened. "That's right. We all have our own—" He fumbled for a word.

Bardo supplied it: "Fortes."

Flip said, "Man, like that's the first time I ever heard it put just that way. Crazy!"

"Keep your eyes on Orion, gentlemen," Raleigh said, "and let the Defenders march on singing!"

In a mood of curious and prodigious camaraderie then, the trio made its way in the night. The summer air was sultry, and busy with the intermittent rumbling of buses along Fifth Avenue, and cars and taxis that took the winding road through the park. Singing, the three went slowly in step along the path, each one now able to quell his peculiar anxiety of the evening, though not forget it. Flip could not forget the fact that he had nowhere to go afterward though his hunger had subsided, the way hunger will when it has gone unsatisfied for too long. Manny could not forget Sincere, and the remaining doubt that his pet belonged there and would not be better back at home, though the doctor and the man he had met a few days ago in the park were blocked out of his thoughts. Bardo could not forget that memory recalled to him so strangely only minutes ago, though the injury of Ivy's running off to eat with McCoy mere *hours* after she had announced her intention of marrying him (callous!) was less painful. The three were more a whole now than they had ever been before, and who was to say the night did not belong to them? In it, there was some open-sesame that would admit them together, it seemed, to their separate roadsteads. All of them, too, were aware that this was only temporary; but instead of making them desperate or uneasy in the face of time, the realization solidifed them and made their togetherness a vaguely triumphant fact. And they had a song; never mind the words .

We'll attack them, and we'll beat them, and upon
them leave our mark,
Then we'll go marching on!

"Hey, man," Flip said when they had paused in their singing, "what's our mark?"

"We ought to have three stars, like in Orion's belt," Manny said.

"Pollack, you're brilliant!" Bardo stated. "Of *course!*"

"Old Manny-man," Flip said, "never know you flunked anything the way you're sounding off t'night." He kicked a rock in the pathway and pulled his hat down on his head more securely.

Manny mumbled, "I just know from Irv." He frowned and held his box more tightly, peeved with Heine for mentioning his failure. He hoped Bardo had not heard; and Bardo hadn't. For suddenly Raleigh stopped in his tracks and held his hand back, halting the other two.

"Hush!" he said. "Hush! Look!" He pointed with his finger. In the darkness ahead of them, a man sat idly on a bench alone, with a bottle tilted to his lips. He was in shirt sleeves; a thin, middle-aged man wearing dark pants, a white handkerchief knotted around his neck soaking up his sweat.

"A goddamned vagrant," Raleigh muttered. "Pardon my obscenity, but look!"

Flip and Manny looked.

Manny said, "He's drinking whisky."

"Right, mister!"

"Just sitting there drinking whisky," Flip said matter-of-factly.

Angrily Raleigh declared, "While his wife and children starve!"

"Do you think so?" Manny asked.

"He probably goes home and beats up his kids," Flip said. "Like, punches them around."

"He's a rat!" Bardo said. "Come on. We'll just pretend to be passing by. Then we'll surround him."

"What'll we do then?" Manny said.

"Come on, gentlemen. This is the first business of the day."

"You mean the night, man."

The three boys walked leisurely toward the bench without talking. The man did not look at them while they came, and when they stopped before him he looked up casually.

"Pop to, mister!" Bardo exclaimed.

"On your feet!" said Flip.

Manny put the box down on the ground.

The man laughed. "Punks!" he said. "Young punks." He took a swig from the bottle, swallowed, and then spat on the ground.

Furiously Bardo said, "Pop to, mister!"

"G'wan home and dry behind your ears, buddy."

"Got your knife, Heine? This vagrant thinks we're kidding."

The blade of Flip's knife flashed in the air, silver and quick.

Manny said, "We aren't going to rob you if you get up."

"Maybe we are and maybe we aren't," Flip said. He pointed the knife at the man menacingly. "Pop to, man!" he said, and Bardo's eyes narrowed on the man.

The man got up. He shoved his bottle into his hip pocket.

Bardo ordered, "Break that bottle, mister. You've had the last of that bottle."

The man grabbed Flip's arm and twisted it back. "Drop your toy, Boy Scout," he grunted. "Drop it on the ground!"

Flip's face twisted with pain.

"Don't hurt him," Manny said.

Flip cried, "C'mon, you guys, help me!"

But Bardo simply stood there, his face white with rage, shaking, shouting, "Vagrant! Dirty vagrant!"

The knife dropped to the ground and the man put his foot on it. He gave Heine a shove. "Punk!" He laughed. "You punk!"

Heine stood there, his head bent, his arms dangling at his sides. Bardo backed away. "You haven't heard the last of us, mister," he threatened. "We'll kill you the next time we see you. We'll kill you!"

Manny said, "Did he hurt you, Flip?"

"Shut up!" Flip answered.

The man walked directly over to Bardo. He took him by the shoulders. Flip just stood watching.

Bardo said, "Take your fool hands off me. This minute!" A vein pulsed in his forehead and his eyes popped with rage.

The man looked at him, still with his hands on Raleigh's shoulders. Then, hawking, he pursed up his lips in a round, fat bow and spat in Bardo's face. He said, "Now run along, Captain Kidd," and he put his hands on his hips and laughed.

Bardo stood transfixed. He was shaking and near to tears. His lips quivered and his teeth were chattering.

"Go on!" the man said. "Get the hell out of here—all of you."

Flip started first, his hands in his pockets, his head lowered. He touched Bardo's arm when he passed him. "Come on," he said. "Let's cut out."

Bardo moved as though he were in a trance, wiping his face now with his clean handkerchief. Manny picked up the box.

As Manny began to follow, the man said, "What are you carrying?"

"A box," Manny said, frightened.

"What's in it?"

"A s-snake," Manny said. Then quickly he said, "Please don't do anything to it, sir. I—"

"I'm not going to do anything to it, Junior." He touched Manny's wrist. "You ought to go home, Junior. You don't belong with these punks."

Manny jumped at the touch.

"What's the matter with you?" the man said.

Manny began to run. "Wait!" he called to the others. "Wait!"

The man looked after them, standing and scratching his neck. He pulled the bottle out and drank. Then he ambled slowly along the pathway into the darkness, away from the trio.

For a long time no one said anything. They came up to Ninety-first Street, where the pathway ended. On one side of them there was the reservoir, and on the other Fifth Avenue. They stopped there and Flip spoke first.

"That was a good knife," he said. "It's back there on the ground."

"Go and get it, mister," Bardo answered.

"You think he's—"

"Are you scared of him, mister? Go and get that knife!"

"Sure," Flip said. "Sure. I—I'll be right back." He sprinted away from Manny and Bardo, and the two stood silently. In the distance a clock chimed ten, and a doorman on Fifth whistled persistently for a taxi.

"You know something funny, Bardo?" Manny said, breaking the silence after several minutes.

"I don't know anything *funny*," Bardo answered.

"Well, I didn't mean funny, exactly," Manny said. "I meant sort of strange. Last week when I was on my way home I cut through the—"

Bardo interrupted. "I'll never forget this, Pollack! Are you aware of that? I'll—never—forget—this!" He stared at the handkerchief wadded up in his hand.

"It was unsanitary to do that. Spit in someone's face."

"Correct, mister! It was *vile!*"

"People shouldn't do things without thinking. You never know how it's going to make the next fellow feel," Manny said. He set his box down and squatted by it. "I ought to see if Sinny's O.K."

"You've got a head on your shoulders, Pollack," Raleigh said. He repeated, *"Vile."*

"Gee, thanks, Bardo. Hi, Sinny! Hi, old boy! He's all curled up under the grass, Bardo." Manny smiled. "I bet next year I won't have any trouble in school. I'm not dumb or anything. It's just . . ." His voice trailed off. He said to the snake, "Go to sleep, pal. No one's going to bother you, pal."

Raleigh stood with his hands clasped behind his back, the handkerchief still rolled up in one of them. He pressed his lips together and rocked back and forth, looking up at the stars.

"O-rion!" he said emphatically. "Slayer of beasts."

"Some animals eat snakes," Manny said, standing up again. "But a snake is smart, too. In *Life* magazine once I saw a picture where a snake actually swallowed a pig. I mean, a little snake swallowing a great big pig!" Manny snickered. "'S funny how smart they are."

"I'll remember his face," Bardo said, "and one day we'll meet again."

Flip returned breathless, brandishing the knife. "I got it!" He grinned. "Where to now?"

"That was a pretty silly idea, mister, cutting your hair off that way," Bardo commented, looking again at Flip in the light.

"Whatsa difference?"

"It might never grow back, Flip," Manny said. "I heard once—"

Flip cut into his words. "Like, I'm tired of hearing all the things you ever heard, Manny-man. Like, what is this? Graduation Day?"

"I just—"

Flip said angrily, "Well, what are we gonna do? Stand around and yak all night? Cripes, let's take off."

"Right, mister!"

"Why don't we take the path around the reservoir? We can cut off down by the bridge," Flip said.

"That little incident," Bardo said as the three shuffled up the cinder path toward the reservoir steps, "is permanently engraved on my memory. *Permanently!*"

"He musta studied ju-jitz or something like that. Cripes, he was no Atlas, man. I mean, ordinarily I could take a guy like that on. But he knew tricks. You know?"

"A vile bully!" Bardo said.

Manny jogged along a little behind them, carrying his box.

It was Pollack that was the first to spy the second man.
Flip and Bardo were ahead of him, going up the stone
steps, and Manny saw the recumbent figure in the grass
under the bushes a little distance from the trio, just off
the bridle path that circled the reservoir.

"Psssst!" Manny called to the two. "Pssst!"

"You a teapot or something crazy, man? You gotta
hiss?"

"Look down there," Manny said. "Guy's asleep down
there."

Bardo's eyes brightened. "Good work!" he said enthusiastically. "Good work, Pollack!" Then he turned and
started down the steps, in the sleeping man's direction.
"Come on," he said.

Flip snapped his knife's blade in and out as he went,
and Manny said to Flip, "I almost didn't see him there."

"You're getting a big head tonight, man," Flip grumbled.
"Pretty soon the dunce cap won't fit it any more."

Manny shut up then; angry, his feelings hurt too. Flip
was needling him too much. Why?

The three approached the man quietly, walking word-
lessly across the parched grass into the small thicket where
he lay. His shoes were off, one lying by the tall elm tree
there, the other under a bush. He wore no socks. He slept
face down, his mouth open, his head cradled in his arms.
His shirt was an old faded blue work shirt, his pants ragged
denims. He slept deeply, wheezing slightly.

"Let's wake him up," Flip said. He started to kneel
near the man and shake him.

"Wait a second," Bardo told him. "I know a better
way." He reached into his pocket and drew out a pack of
cigarettes, tapping one out and lighting it.

"You smoke, huh, Bardo?" Manny said. He put his box
down and looked at Bardo as he lit the cigarette. "I didn't
know that."

Flip said, "Man, like, what'd you think?"

"No, I don't smoke, mister," Bardo said coolly. "It's a
filthy habit." He sucked on the cigarette to get it going.
"Mr. McCoy left this little memento behind on our hall
table. I thought it might very well be of some use."

"He was crazy!" Flip said. "I liked him."

Bardo looked at Heine with a cocked eyebrow. "That's
very touching, Herr Heine," he said. "Very touching in-
deed."

"I wish you'd lay off the Herr," Flip said, "You know, man?"

Manny laughed suddenly. "Yeah, because he doesn't have any. Huh, Flip?"

"A clever play on words, Pollack," Bardo said. "Now let's attend to business." As he knelt down in the grass with the lighted cigarette, Heine stood rocklike, scowling at Pollack, making his knife blade pop in and out. Manny felt Flip's eyes fixed on him. He knew Flip was sore at him.

"Watch this," Bardo said.

He took the lighted cigarette and brought it slowly up to the sleeping man's bare foot; then he held it to the sole, and it burned the flesh a second.

"Jesus!" The man jerked his foot away. He exclaimed, "Jesus, what the—" He blinked his eyes and raised himself on his elbows. He said, "What's going on?"

He was about fifty, a medium-sized man with straggly white hair. In the darkness his face was not too clear, but his expression of astonishment was. His eyes were screwed up in a squint, his lips curled to one side and open. His voice was husky with sleep.

"Pop to!" Bardo snapped. "Pop to, mister! On your feet!"

"Huh?" the man just blinked like a lazy mud turtle on a rock in the sun. "Huh?"

Flip kicked him in the side. "Get up, man!" he said.

Manny said, "He smells like he's been drinking, too."

"He smells foul!" Bardo said, "Now, mister, I tell you to pop,"—he kicked him once in the gut—"to!" He kicked him in the hip.

The man groaned. "Whata you want? Ooooh! God!" He tried to get up, but he could not. He was very drunk, and now he was dazed, unable to comprehend what was happening to him.

Bardo said, "Get him on his feet, Heine. Help him, Pollack."

The two boys raised the man up. He was only a little taller than Bardo. "Drunk!" Bardo spat the word out. He went to the man and slapped him hard across the face; three times, four, five. "Drunk!"

The man began to sober up some. He shook his head. "Where am I?"

"You're nowhere, man."

"You're in Central Park," Manny said.

"Who are you? What the hell's going on?" The man yanked himself free, stumbled, but stood, and Flip took his arm again.

Bardo was looking around behind him and to the right and left of him. He said, "We've got a good safe place."

The man began to yell. "Help! Hel—"

Bardo put a fist in his stomach and he toppled back on the ground. Bardo straddled him, sitting on his stomach. Flip knelt down with his knife pointed.

"We don't want any noise, mister," Bardo said. "We don't like noise."

"What do you want from me?" the man said.

"Man, like, we're going to give you a little instruction. Yeah."

"A lesson," Bardo said. "A lesson you'll never forget."

"Come on, boys," the man said. "I'm old enough to be your father. Have a heart, boys."

Flip took a handful of dried grass and dirt from the ground, cupped it in his hand, and held it to the old man's mouth. "Have some dinner, Pop," he said. "Specially prepared. Specialty of the house." He brought the knife in nearer to the man's face. "Eat it, Pop!" he said. "Eat your dinner!" and he shoved it in the man's mouth. The man spat it out.

Bardo said, "He—told—you—to—eat—that—mister!" Bardo's eyes glistened. "Roll him over on his stomach. Come on, Pollack. Don't just stand there staring like a dummy."

"I'm *not!*" Manny said. He bent over and, with Flip, rolled the man over.

"Please," the man said, "I'm not well. I'm not at all well, boys."

"Shut your yap," Flip said. He pulled the old man's hair. "Shut your yap or we'll burn this here off your head, Pop!"

"What are you going to do now?" Manny asked.

"Get his pants down, Pollack."

"Why?"

"Pollack, do as Bardo Raleigh tells you."

Manny put his hands under the man and grappled with the belt. Flip held the knife to his ear. "One word out of you, Pop," he said, "you'll eat your ear for breakfast."

"Boys, have some mercy," the man said.

"I'm warning you, Pop."

Manny pulled the man's pants below his knees. Flip sat on the man's back, his hands around his throat, the knife stuck in his belt. "All I got to do is squeeze, Pop, if you decide to sound off."

"All right, Pollack," Bardo said. "Find me a good strong stick. A big one. A thick piece of wood. Meanwhile, the three stars of Orion's belt." He knelt between the man's legs, taking another cigarette from his pocket and lighting it. "Heine, you holding him?"

"Yeah, man!"

"Heine, I want you to sing along with me now. You hear? Sing soft, but don't let any other noise from here drown us out!"

"Got it!" Heine said.

"Hold him good, Heine. . . . O.K. Mine eyes have seen the vagrants on the benches in the park . . ."

As they sang, and the old man struggled to be free and wiggled with pain, calling out once, "Help!" Bardo burned three marks in a row on his rump.

"Cut!" he said. "That's enough singing until Pollack gets back."

The old man was crying now, sniffling and moaning.

The figure of a man in the distance, coming around the reservoir, caught Raleigh's eye. "Get his pants up, Heine. Fast!" he said. "Get him on his feet, and back farther in the bushes. Do you see?"

"Yeah," Heine said. He did as he was told; and as the two dragged him back into the bushes and held him, Manny came with the stick.

"I couldn't find one much better," he said.

"Get in here, Pollack," Bardo said, "and never mind."

The trio crouched there holding the man down, waiting until the passer-by went on far beyond them.

The old man sobbed to himself. Flip slapped him and said, "Shut up."

Manny said, "Maybe we ought to let him go."

"Not until he's had his lesson, mister."

"He's crying," Manny said.

Flip said, "Pollack, you are beginning to get me very rifty, man. Like, I really am getting very rifty at you!"

"Well, he's awful old," Manny said.

"Mister, he's no good. He's a bum!" Bardo pounded the man's back. "A bum!"

"You gonna use the stick, or can I?" Flip said.

"You can, Heine. Everybody better sing. Come on— Glory, glory, hallelujah! Glory, glory—"

Heine raised the stick and swatted it across the old man.

"He ought to be bare-assed," he said. "Like he was before. He could feel it more."

"Christ!" the man yelled.

"Sing," Raleigh said. "Sing!" And then he said suddenly, "Stop! Listen!" They heard the crunch of footsteps on the cinder bridle path. "Quiet," Bardo said. "Don't make a move"; and the old man yelled, "Help!"

Flip drove the knife part way into his shoulders. The old man made a throaty gagging noise, and Manny said, "Hey, Flip!"

"Shut up, all of you!" Bardo commanded.

Then on the path in front of them they saw John Wylie.

"Hey, it's Wyle!" Flip said. "Wyle, c'mere." Flip yanked and got the knife out. He said, "I just *did* it. I didn't mean to. It didn't hurt him much."

"He asked for it," Bardo said.

"Hey, Wyle," Manny said. "Flip just knifed a guy."

Johnny Wylie walked over to where the man lay, with Flip on top of him.

"Hi!" Flip said.

"What'd you do, Flip?"

"I just nicked him, 's all. Just a little nick. Pollack makes out like I was killing the old fool."

"He's bleeding," Johnny said.

"He's all right!" Bardo asserted. "He's all right!"

"Help me," the old man moaned. "Help me."

Angrily Raleigh kicked him in the face. He kicked him again and again, so hard that the crack of his shoe across the skin and bone sounded unbelievably loud. Manny sucked in his breath and Johnny flinched.

Flip said, "*Grüss Gott!*"

Bardo looked at the three of them. "What's the matter?" he said. "Haven't you even seen a man discipline a man? Haven't you?" he shouted.

The old man did not move much now; only once or twice. Blood poured from his face; his features were blurred with it.

"He needs help," Johnny said dazedly. "Somebody ought to go for—"

"We could call an ambulance," Manny said.

"You gentlemen are exceedingly clever, both of you," Bardo said. "Go for *help!* Call an *ambulance!* He's scum—pure scum!"

"Yeah, like, he was loaded, Johnny. You know? Drunk? Lying around."

"He was sleeping on the grass," Manny said.

"He looks like he's going to die. My God, he does!" John Wylie said. "I'm going for help."

"Remember, mister," Raleigh said to him, "you're involved in this too. Remember that before you call for help!"

"I am like hell involved!"

"You came to join us, didn't you, mister?"

"I knew you were around here someplace. Then I heard you singing. I didn't know what you were doing."

"You were with us last week, mister."

"Look," Johnny said. "I'm going for help."

Flip said, "Wyle?"

"What?"

"You're not going to the police, Wyle?"

"Naw. Naw—I'll get a priest. I'll get Father Farrell." Johnny looked at the trio, frowning. He said, "Father Farrell's O.K. I mean, he won't have to know how it happened. Why don't you guys just clear out? If there's any trouble—" Johnny stopped in the middle of the sentence, his eyes falling again to the old man on the ground. "I'm getting out of here!" Johnny said.

Raleigh and Heine and Pollack stood staring at the old man.

Bardo Raleigh said, "Now we are all murderers."

"Grüss Gott!" Flip said. *"Grüss Gott!"*

"Is he dead?" Manny said. "Are you sure?"

"On the double," Raleigh barked. "Let's *go!*"

Then the three boys ran.

16

Emanuel Pollack, son of a Manhattan jeweler and younger brother of a dead Korean war hero, was described by police as being more concerned over the welfare of a pet snake . . . than he was over the condition of his victim.
—*New York Daily Record*

THE FOUR POLICEMEN stood over the body with flashlights in their hands while Father Farrell knelt and prayed. John Wylie stood to one side, his head bowed.

"*Misereatur vestri omnipotens Deus, et dimissis peccatis vestris, preducat vos ad vitam aeternam. Amen.*"

The priest rose. "May God grant him eternal rest," he said.

"We'd appreciate it, Father, if you'd come along with us," a policeman said. "You and the boy."

John Wylie said, "I don't know anything about it. Honest."

"How come a kid like you wanders around here this time of night?" the policeman said.

"I don't know. I was just—walking."

Father Farrell put his arm around Wylie. "We'll go along with them, Johnny, and try to help them if we can."

"I can't help them, Father.. I can't."

Another policeman said, "Ever see this, sonny?"

In his hand he held Flip's switchblade knife. There was blood on it; it was lying on top of the policeman's white handkerchief. Johnny winced.

"Well?"

"No," Johnny said.

"What were you doing back in these bushes?" another policeman asked.

Johnny said, "I don't remember. I don't know."

"You come along with us," the policeman said. He turned to the three men with him. "O'Connor and I'll go with the kid and Father Farrell. You stay here."

128

"Right."

"Looks fishy to me."

"Right."

"Check the ground, back in behind the shrubbery."

The policeman said, "Shall we go now, Father?"

"Come along, Johnny," the priest said, with his arm still around the boy. "Everything will be all right."

"Please don't call my family," Johnny said. "Please."

The policeman didn't answer; they walked ahead of Johnny and the priest. Just as they were rounding the curve in the cinder path, they saw a second boy running toward them. He was breathless, and when they grabbed him he said, "No, please. Please. First just let me look on the ground."

Johnny said, "Manny!"

"Sincere," Manny said. "I forgot about him. I left him here."

"You were here, kid?" the policeman asked.

Manny said, "He's in a box. Just let me look."

"You come with us," the policeman said. He held Pollack's wrists.

"Please," Manny said, "let me get the box first. It's around here someplace."

"Yeah? What's in it?"

"My snake," Manny said.

Johnny shook his head. "Manny," he said. "Manny . . . oh, God!"

"If anyone finds your snake they'll bring him along," the policeman said. "Don't worry about that. Come on. Both of you kids have got some explaining to do."

Manny tried to twist free. "Let me get my snake first!" he shouted.

"Do you know the boy, Johnny?" Father Farrell asked Wylie.

"Yes, Father," Johnny said quietly.

The two policemen held Emanuel Pollack. "All right," one said, "come on! Move!"

"Please?" Manny begged.

"Move!"

Crying then, Emanuel Pollack was led along by the two policemen. Following behind, the priest and Johnny Wylie walked slowly.

"You'd better tell them all you know, Johnny," Father Farrell whispered in the darkness.

And so on August 10, 1953, the *New York Daily Record* spread this story across its front page:

FOUR BOYS ADMIT SLAYING
JUST FOR FUN

Four teen-agers who stormed through upper Central Park, killing and attacking for pleasure, confessed last night to the wanton murder of one man, the sadistic undressing of a young girl, and the savage beating of the girl's boy friend.

The leader of the Murder for Fun gang exulted that they called themselves "The Defenders," and that their purpose was to rid the parks of bums and vagrants. Words to a song proclaiming this sentiment were found in his pocket.

"Bardo Raleigh has an infinite hatred and loathing for bums and filthy vagrants," the leader of the four, Bardo Raleigh, 17, was quoted as saying.

A youth with an exceptionally high I.Q. and a recent graduate of Sandside Military Academy in Sandside, Georgia, Raleigh bossed the operations while Hans Heine, 16, a junior at Eastern High School, did the dirty work, police said.

"Last night was Raleigh's revenge," Raleigh reportedly said. He was referring, police said, to the beating and stabbing of 57-year-old Milton Litt, homeless, who died of cerebral hemorrhage and/or a heart attack.

"Robbery was not the motive for this crime," New York Attorney Robert Evans said. "I can't fathom what would make boys do this sinister and horrible thing."

Raleigh and Heine, together with John Wylie, 15, and snake-lover Emanuel Pollack, 16, started their club with their first crime spree August 2, Evans said. On that date the four attacked Carlos Rodriguez and Linda Torres on a Central Park pathway, forcing Miss Torres to disrobe and beating Rodriguez. . . .

Last night the four again invaded Central Park, searching for a likely victim. The homeless Milton Litt, asleep on the grass with his shoes off, became their prey. . . .

After the attack, Litt was left to die while Wylie, "baby" of the quartet, went conscience-stricken to a priest for help.

Emanuel Pollack, son of a Manhattan jeweler and younger brother of a dead Korean war hero, was described by police as being more concerned over the welfare of a pet snake he had left at the scene of the crime than he was over the condition of his victim. It was his sudden appearance, while police, Wylie, and Father Thomas Farrell returned to the spot where Litt lay dead, that forced Wylie to admit his link with the crime, and subsequently forced a confession from Pollack. The young killer had come back to get his snake.

Acting on information gained from these two members of the kill-for-thrill club, Detective Lawrence Littlefield went to find Raleigh and Heine. Heine was picked up on Fifth Avenue between 80th and 81st Streets, curled up on a bench asleep. An envelope filled with marijuana was found in his pocket. Raleigh was arrested at his home.

Raleigh, Heine, and Pollack were charged with homicide, and Wylie was charged with juvenile delinquency growing out of homicide. . . .

17.

Investigation of the backgrounds of the four youths established that they are from respectable families.
—*New York Daily Record*

In the interrogation room his father was standing near the door. When Johnny came in, he stood awkwardly before him, unable to look him in the eye. He said nothing. Then Richard Wylie put his arm around the boy's shoulder.

"It's all right, son," he said.

"I'm sorry, Dad."

"Do you want to tell me about it, John?"

"I didn't do it, Dad," he said. "I wasn't even there when it happened."

"Neither time, John?"

"The first time I was," Johnny said. "But it wasn't like they say. We didn't make that girl take all her clothes off. Just her blouse and stuff." Johnny looked shamefacedly at the floor. "Bardo was the one who kicked the boy."

"You didn't touch the boy or the girl, then?"

"The girl," Johnny mumbled.

"You did something to the girl, son?"

"No! I mean I just—you know, I felt of her b-breast."

"I see." Richard Wylie sighed and walked over to sit down on the bench near the window. He shook his head slowly. "And then?" he said.

"Nothing. I just—did that, and that was all."

"You just felt her breast. Period."

Johnny said, "Oh, God, Dad! I feel like some kind of maniac. A sex maniac or something."

"Is that all you did, son?"

"Yes, sir. I don't know why. . . . I don't know. This summer I've been thinking about things a lot. I've been thinking about—girls. I just don't know."

"Go on, John. Tell me the rest."

Johnny stood holding onto the back of a chair, not facing his father.

132

"The other night, sir," he said, "I lied. I said I was taking Lynn Leonard to a movie. Well, we weren't going to a movie. We—we were going up on the roof."

"Why did you lie about that?"

"Because we were going to— I can't talk about it, Dad."

"I think I understand."

"Anyway, she didn't show. I was sore or something. I wanted to go off. I remembered Bardo saying the gang was meeting up by the children's park, up at Ninety-sixth, so I just went."

"And then?"

"I was late. When I got there it had already happened."

"You're sure of that, John?"

Johnny whirled around. "Don't you believe me?" he shouted.

"Easy," his father said. "Just calm down, young man."

"Thrill-killers," Johnny said. "That's what they're calling us. They brought a paper to us, and that's what it said. And all this stuff about a club. What club? I didn't even know about it!"

"Look, son," his father said. "If you are innocent—and I believe you, by the way—then you'll be cleared. But some of the dirt's going to rub off on you, son. You've got to be prepared for that."

"I know it, Dad. I know it."

"Now let's go over everything in detail. That's why I insisted that your mother stay home, so we could get everything straight. Start from the very beginning, and don't be ashamed to tell me about the girls. O.K.?"

"All right," Johnny said.

As he talked, John Wylie had the odd sensation that he was talking about some other person. It was the same as when he had read the newspapers that morning. He felt sorry for Manny. Manny had cried all night over the snake. Bardo Raleigh had comforted him, his calm voice prevailing throughout the hours until dawn.

"That's all right, mister. They won't hurt that snake. Your snake will be fine."

None of it seemed real to Johnny.

And Lynn Leonard . . . Johnny couldn't even see her face on the screen of his memory any more, or recall the sound of her voice. But sometimes he could swear he could smell the lilacs; he could swear he could. And the ache in him would begin. He would think of how he had waited,

of how it might have been if she had come; how different
from the way it was. He thought of her reading the newspapers, reading the part about the girl they said had been
forced to take her clothes off, and inside of him he died,
only to be resurrected again and given his choice of night-
mares.

When Johnny finished telling his father about it, he was
sobbing.

"That's about it, Dad," he said.

Richard Wylie walked across the interrogation room
and took hold of his son's shoulders. "It was a mistake,
son. It was a big mistake."

"I know it, Dad."

"Thank God you weren't involved in the murder."

"I keep thanking God," Johnny said. "I keep asking
Him to forgive me."

"I'll be back tomorrow, John. Along with your mother.
By the way," he said, fumbling in his suit pocket, "she
wrote you a little note. And here's another one." He
handed them to Johnny. Then he hugged the boy to him.
"You're our boy, John," he said. "We wouldn't want any
other boy but you."

Johnny wept until the guard came.

Back in the single cell they had assigned him that
morning, he opened the note from his mother:

Dearest Son,

I'll come to see you tomorrow. Meanwhile pray to
God for courage, and remember that your father and I
love you and believe in you.

Mom

The second note was from Lynn Leonard, and it said:

Dear Johnny,

I still mean everything I said last Thursday night.
Remember? Honestly! No matter what the papers print.
I don't believe it. Johnny, I *couldn't* come that night. I
can't tell you why I couldn't, but please believe me.
Maybe someday I can tell you. I wanted to come,
Johnny. I just *couldn't.* Try to understand. I lit a candle
for you at St. Mary's. Oh, Johnny, please don't hate me.
I love you.

Lynn

A guard rattled Johnny's cell door, opening it. "O.K., Mr. Big Kicks," he said. "The D.A.'s got a few more questions. Put away the fan mail, Mr. Thrill."

The office was comfortable. The desk was large, with papers scattered on top, and a few books. A package of cigarettes was open and two ash trays were filled with butts.

The doctor looked up at Heine. He was standing framed by the window behind him; he held a report in his hand.

"Hans Heine?"

His eyes were cool, neither kindly nor condemning.

"Yeah."

"I'm Dr. Wetman. Sit down, Hans."

Heine sat down and braced his hands on his thighs.

"Relax, Hans. We're just going to chat." He took a cigarette from the pack and offered the pack to Heine. "Smoke?" he said.

"I don't smoke or drink," Heine answered.

The doctor's voice was not cold, and he smiled at Flip. "Not even marijuana?" he said.

"Naw," Flip said. "I just had that for a gag."

"Your folks were here an hour or so ago, weren't they, Hans?"

Flip said, "Uh-huh."

He hated to remember the scene in the interrogation room. His mother had looked shabby and old and out of place there, and suddenly she had looked very little to Flip too, and pathetic. She had not been able to stop crying; she had cried the whole time, making any conversation between them virtually impossible. But his father had talked to Flip. His father had said he had warned Flip that something like this would happen; he had warned him, hadn't he? His father had wanted to know how Flip thought the whole family felt with his picture on the front page of the *Daily Record*. His father had said, "Are you satisfied now, Hans, that you have dragged our good name in the mud?"

"How did it go?" Dr. Wetman asked.

"Rough."

"Why, Hans?"

"Man, like, they just never did dig me. You know?"

The doctor nodded.

"I mean I'm an American."

"Yes," the doctor said.

"I couldn't even read comic books. What kid doesn't read comic books? All American kids do."

The doctor reached for something on his desk. He handed it to Heine. It was a battered copy of *Night of Horror*.

"Is this the sort of thing you read?"

"That's it. Only, like, not all the time, man," Flip added unsurely, afraid now of what this man would think of him.

"I notice," the doctor said, "in this one they have several characters carrying switchblade knives."

"Yeah. They go in big for that."

"You had a knife like that, didn't you?"

Flip said, "Yeah. That's the knife I used. Police took it."

"Do the others read these comics, Hans?"

"Didn't you ask them?"

"I'm not examining them," Wetman said. "I asked Judge McKeon to let me talk with you a few times before the trial."

"Why me?" Flip said. Then his hand went to his shorn head. "My head, huh? Because I shaved off my hair for a gag? Like, I'm crazy or something?"

"You see, the main reason for an examination," Wetman said, "is to determine a point of legal sanity or insanity. The doctor you talked with yesterday was in charge of that."

"And I'm nuts, huh? I told him how my head happened."

"I know, Hans. No, you're not nuts. No, you see, I'm interested in discovering what attraction these comic books have for young people. I'm informed you're something of an authority."

Flip grinned. "Man, like, I must of read millions, I guess."

"And you like what in particular about them?"

"Oh, you know—all those knives sticking out of people's middles." Flip laughed, and at the same time he wondered why he had said it. He wanted the doctor to be interested in him, to want to talk with him. It was funny; the doctor was a foreigner too—he had an accent—but Flip liked him. Why had he liked him so immediately? There was something about his mildness.

"Is that all?"

"Nobody gets pushed around."

"Nobody?"

"You know, man. Like, in one this guy started shoving this kid around, and the kid came back that night with some other kids and they made the guy dance to music. You know? They were whipping his legs."

"Hmmm."

"You can get a whip for three-seventy-five," Flip said. "They advertise them."

"Did you ever send away for one?"

"Naw. Like, who needs it?"

Flip fumbled with his hands. It was curious; he was thinking of a song, the one with which his sister always opened the second set at the place. *"Du Lieblicher Stern.* He had been humming it to himself all day and remembering the way his mother always sighed and said, *"Ach, du schönes Deutschland!"*

"What are you smiling at, Hans?"

"Was I smiling?"

"Yes."

Heine shrugged his shoulders. "I don't know," he said. "Let's talk about comic books."

The doctor nodded. "All right."

"Well," Flip began, "in one there's this bat man and his friend. I mean, this bat man really digs his friend, you know? He takes care of him and everything. He's older, like, a lot older, and they hang around together. I remember in one," Flip continued . . .

He wondered as he talked if he could keep the doctor sufficiently interested in him to want to see him a second time. Manny and Johnny and Bardo had their folks coming every day, coming and bringing them things. His folks wouldn't be back, Flip felt. And then in the back of his mind the little poem his mother had spoken played over and over like a broken record:

> *Schön ist's vielleicht anderswo*
> *Doch hier sind wir sowieso.*

"Man," Flip said in a burst of desperate, feigned enthusiasm, "the comic books are the craziest! The things those cats think up. Like, in one there was this doll getting herself whipped and then . . ."

The guard led him through the block past the cells and up into the interrogation room. He walked in step with the guard and turned square corners. At the door of the interrogation room he saluted the guard. "O.K., General," he said. "P'toon dis-*missed!*"

He was smiling when he walked in. Ivy Raleigh stood looking at him, saying, "Bar! Bar!" He went to her and they embraced.

"Ummmm!" he said. "Arpège?"

"Chanel," she answered mechanically, studying his face carefully.

"Now, Ivy," he said. "I told you not to worry."

"But in the papers, Bar—they quote you as saying all those things."

"Ivy, I told you yesterday. This is all trumped up! I wasn't even with those infantile people. Leogrande will prove that at the trial."

"Bar, even if the truth is terrible, won't you tell me? Please, Bar, it's important!"

"Ivy," he said solemnly, looking into her eyes, "Bardo has never lied to you, has he?"

"No, darling," she answered. She paced across the room, clutching her hands together. "Some of the quotes, though, Bar. They sound like you. You know, the way you use the third person? And you never did like bums. I'm just so— Oh, Bar, darling, darling—please tell me if you had anything to do with it!" She stood there, her hands outstretched toward her son.

"You look lovely," Bardo said. "New dress?"

"No."

"Perfect color for you. Bardo approves." He smiled at her. "Ivy, dear, relax. I'll be out of here in no time, and there'll be some apologies from the authorities, you can bet. You know, John Wylie's getting out. Well, I will too." He took her hands. "I'm innocent, Ivy. This is all trumped up—all of it. You can thank your United Press for that! You have your eminent newsmen to thank for that!"

She dropped her hands from his and sat down on the bench. "But where were you, Bar? Where were you that night? You've never made it clear. Ernest can't help you if you don't confide in him."

"Ivy, I was at the movies. I told you that."

"No, Bar. You didn't. You said—oh, darling, you said you were home."

"I *was* home. Then I went to the movies. I went to see *The Conquest of Everest* at the Trans-lux on Madison. There now, are you satisfied? Really, Ivy. You do believe Bardo?"

"I want to, Bar. My baby." She rested her face in her hands.

Bardo strolled about the room with his hands in his pockets. "You know," he said, "the latrines in this place are kept in an infinitely filthy condition."

"Bar, Bar—" She watched him walk back and forth.

"Poor Pollack," he said. "He's a nice lad. I'm sorry he's mixed up in this."

"Is that Emanuel?"

"Yes."

"The one with the snake?"

"Yes. Sincere," Raleigh said. "Wonderful creature."

Ivy looked more carefully at Bardo. He was rubbing something between his fingers. The sun caught the reflection and sent a dart of light to the ceiling.

She said, "Bar, what's that in your hand?"

He looked down at the ring. "Your ring," he said. He smiled at her. "I found it. I was going to surprise you."

"Bar, in the papers they—" Tears came to her eyes, and her words came with difficulty. "They said that Carlos Rodriguez had to kiss a—" She could not finish the sentence. Bardo Raleigh ran to her.

"No, Ivy," he said. "Don't cry! Bardo can't bear to see you cry, Ivy. Listen, Ivy, those reporters are liars! Infinite liars, Ivy!"

"My poor, poor darling," she said.

"McCoy!" Bardo Raleigh said. "He never liked me, Ivy. He never did." He knelt by her, looking up at her. "He was jealous, Ivy."

"Yes, Bar, yes," she said through her tears. She put her hand on his head, running her fingers gently through his hair. "Yes, my darling," she said.

"You believe me, don't you, Ivy?" he asked.

"All right, Bar. Yes. Yes."

"And you won't—you won't marry him, will you, Ivy?"

"Oh, Bar!" she cried.

"Promise," he insisted. "Promise."

"I won't marry him," Ivy Raleigh said.

Bardo smiled broadly. "Huzzah!" he said. "Huzzah! Huzzah!"

"Well," Emanuel Pollack said to his parents in the interrogation room, "tomorrow's the big day, I guess."

His father said, "I guess so."

Pollack sat between them on the bench. His mother was weeping quietly into a handkerchief. She said, "My son! My little boy!"

"Don't cry, Mom," he said. "Gee—don't cry."

"You're just a child!" she said.

"Almost seventeen," he answered. He grinned. "Too young to tango." Where had he heard that? he wondered. Who was it that had said that?

"Are they treating you all right, Emanuel?" his father asked.

"Sure," Manny said. "We had corned beef and cabbage for lunch."

"I brought you some more candy bars," his father said, "in the basket. I brought your *Geographic* too."

"Thanks, Dad. That's swell."

They sat there silently then, save for Ruth Pollack's occasional sobs. Finally Manny said, "Will you tell me again, Dad, about Sincere?"

"If anything happens," his father began, and his mother gave a loud sob, "Sincere will be taken to the Bronx Zoo. They'll give him the very best care in the world up there. They'll know all the things to do for him, you know. That's their business."

"Sure," Manny said. "Sure."

"He'll be in good hands, Emanuel."

"I know it," Pollack said.

The guard's rapping came at the door. "Time's up!"

"Already?" Nathan Pollack said. "Where does the time go?"

His mother hugged him. He raised a hand to put it around her thin shoulders, but dropped it, unable to touch her. "Aw, Mom," he said. "Maybe it'll come out O.K. Maybe."

Mr. Pollack stood up. He shook his head sadly. "We've done everything we could, Emanuel."

"I know it," Manny said.

"I don't know how it happened. You were a good kid. I just don't know."

His mother still hugged him, clutching him tightly.

Manny said, "Well, it did. That's all, I guess."

"You should have listened to the psychologist, Emanuel," his father said. "You should have let her help you."

Manny hung his head. "She never said much, Dad."

"You're just a baby," his mother said, "and they're going to take you away."

The guard opened the door. "Time's up!" he repeated.

Manny stood up. His mother and father looked at him, and he looked at the floor. "Well," he said. "I guess I'll see you tomorrow. In court. I'll see you," he said. He started to go with the guard. His mother reached out and touched him. Her voice was dull and apathetic, as though she were talking in her sleep. Her fingers clutched the sleeve of Manny's coat, then dropped to her side.

She said, "I remember the day your brother and I went to buy that suit. Afterward we ate chow mein in Long-champs, and saw *The Big Sleep*. Humphrey Bogart was in it."

18

THE THRILL IS GONE

*—New York Daily Record headline,
November 29, 1953*

Two Thrill-Killers Sentenced to Life;
Judge Bars Possibility of Parole

CONVICTED THRILL KILLERS Bardo Raleigh, 17, and Hans Heine, 17, today were sentenced to life in prison, without possibility of parole.

Judge R. F. McKeon pronounced sentence on the pair after hearing an abject plea for mercy from Heine, marijuana-carrying "hepcat" of the gang, who celebrated his seventeenth birthday in jail last month.

In a note read to the court by John Ready, counsel supplied by the state for Heine's defense, Heine said he realized now that he had brought disgrace on his family, but declared that he had never meant to be "a bad boy."

"I always wanted to be good; to belong. I never did anything bad before. Not like this. I never dreamed I would end up this way. I never meant to kill that old man," Heine wrote.

The two young killers were found guilty October 14 of first-degree murder in the killing of homeless Milton Litt, a Manhattan vagrant they found in Central Park. Litt was tortured and then left to die.

The jury recommended mercy, but Judge McKeon could have disregarded the recommendation and sentenced the defendants to the electric chair.

As Heine and Raleigh were brought handcuffed to the courtroom, Mrs. Thornton Raleigh, only parent present, had to be taken from the spectators' section in hysterics.

Handcuffs were removed from the two youths during the proceedings, with four Department of Correction guards standing by. The defendants, with their attorneys, were summoned to the bench, and Judge McKeon asked if they had anything to say.

Attorney Ernest Leogrande, representing Raleigh, made an impassioned plea for mercy, declaring that neither boy had received a fair trial. "In this case I ask for an investigation of those who connived to try this case in the press," Leogrande said. "This case was tried in the press! Is this justice? It is heartbreaking to know what Mrs. Raleigh has gone through—what my client has suffered, emotionally and physically. There was no intent to kill! My client is a sick boy!"

In sentencing the pair, Judge McKeon said he had made an exhaustive study of all the aspects of the case, and had decided to accept the jury's recommendation of mercy.

"This means that in the event the Appellate Court should ultimately affirm this judgment of conviction," he said, "you can never be eligible for parole. The only possibility of your ever securing your liberty is through a pardon by the Governor. I hereby sentence each of you to life imprisonment in a state institution."

Heine bent over and wept.

Raleigh, his face wooden, remained standing, gazing blankly at Judge McKeon.

The pair was handcuffed and led from the court. Heine regained his composure somewhat, but Raleigh skipped to get in step with Heine and the attendant officer, and displayed all of his old cockiness as he cut square corners on his way from the courtroom.

In the corridor outside the courtroom, Mrs. Raleigh collapsed upon hearing the sentence.

During the trial the State dropped its first-degree murder charge against John Wylie, 15, "baby" of the quartet, who was not involved in the murder.

Earlier this month Emanuel Pollack, 16, was committed to an institution for delinquent children after Children's Court Justice E. K. Pitts turned down his plea that he be allowed to return home and go back to school.

(Pictures on page 1)

THE END
of a novel by
Vin Packer